BROKEN LIVES

KENNETH N. PRICE

Published in Australia by Sid Harta Books & Print Pty Ltd,
ABN: 34632585293
23 Stirling Crescent, Glen Waverley, Victoria 3150 Australia
Telephone: +61 3 9560 9920
E-mail: author@sidharta.com.au

First published in Australia 2021
This edition published 2021
Copyright © Kenneth N Price 2021
Cover design, typesetting: WorkingType (www.workingtype.com.au)

This book is a work of fiction. Any similarities to that of people
living or dead are purely coincidental.

Kenneth N Price
Broken Lives
ISBN: 9781925707663
pp180

Kenneth Price is a retired Vietnam veteran. When he was seventeen, he enlisted into the Australian Army and was trained as a medic. He was sent to Vietnam in 1968 and worked in a field ambulance and field hospital. His grandfather served in the 9th Battalion in France from 1916 to 1918, and his father served in the Australian Army during WWII. Kenneth's uncle also served as a bomber pilot in WWII and was shot down and killed in 1944. After returning from Vietnam, Kenneth married and went to university where he graduated with Distinction in an Arts Degree, majoring in History and Literature. He also has a Bachelor of Education and a Masters (with Distinction) in Australian Political History. Kenneth spent fourteen years teaching History and English at Brisbane Grammar School and eight years as a lecturer in English in Singapore, where he helped his students obtain their 'O' and 'A' levels from Cambridge University. Writing has always been his passion, and following retirement he was inspired to research his family's military history. This led to writing his first book, *Broken Lives*, which covers some of the exploits of his grandfather's 9th Battalion. Kenneth has six children and ten grandchildren. He is currently married to his second wife and lives in Hervey Bay, Queensland.

Dedicated to my grandfather,
John Herbert Delacour

This photo was taken at the end of WWI. My grandfather is the one seated second from the right. It is one of my favourite photos of him, because it shows he still retained his sense of humour despite having endured the horror that was WWI. I don't know too much about the photo other than that, for this photo, he and his mate exchanged their uniforms for civilian clothes with two French men they had met on leave. Does this suggest what was on their minds at the time— that they would soon be civilians and needed to get used to wearing civilian clothes again?

This book is not a work of biography. This is not my grandfather's story, although he did participate in all the battles described in the book, and some others that are not covered here.

Sergeant Williams knelt on a duckboard lining the bottom of the trench, with one knee down and the other upright. There were seven men altogether waiting to go over the sandbagged top. They were to carry out barbed wire entanglement work, where a German bombardment had made significant gaps in the barricade, which now had to be repaired. Four men carried two sets of barbed wire coils, through which a timber plank had been inserted. Another man carried several steel poles with a circle of steel on top. The poles were individually wrapped in hessian bags to stop any noise that would come from them striking each other. The last man in the group was Lieutenant Bowen, who had recently been promoted from sergeant. He had worked his way up through the ranks, having seen action in Ypres, Bullecourt and the Somme. Two of his men were the latest reinforcements from Australia, and he would have to keep an eye on them, but for now he went over in his mind what he had been told to achieve in this mission.

There were two gaps directly to the left and right of their current position that had to be left free of wire, because these gaps would channel and concentrate attacking forces into a killing zone where enfilade fire from two water-cooled Vickers heavy machine guns could provide continuous crossfire.

Any other gaps in the wire were to be plugged with a random tangled mess approach, by simply pushing together the new wire with the old and tapping in some steel poles where needed. The barbed wire entanglement in front of the trench was already several metres thick and had been repaired many times since the start of the war. The enemy artillery fire blew holes in the entanglement, so that after repairing it had become deeper and deeper and had no consistent pattern to it.

As Lieutenant Bowen stood waiting to move out, the sergeant went through what to do with his men, paying particular attention to the new arrivals.

'If a flare goes up, remember to just freeze in an upright position. If you fall down, your movement will attract enemy fire and we will be stuck out there all night or worse. And remember to keep one eye closed so we can get back to work quickly. Any questions?'

'Yeah. Where are we going, Sarge?'

'Take your directions from the lieutenant. Any other questions?'

The men went quiet, so Lieutenant Bowen rolled over the sandbags and pushed forward in a crouched position. The others followed.

'Fill the gap here, Sergeant,' Lieutenant Bowen whispered.

The men went about their work quickly and quietly. They joined one end of the roll of barbed wire to a loose end of the hole, then stretched it out and cut it at the other end. The click of the cut seemed to echo through the night and they all froze, suspecting a flare to go up from the German position. No flare eventuated, so they continued working. The steel poles that went in to hold the wire in place were tapped into position with the timber poles. The hessian-covered poles produced a muffled sound—but a sound, nonetheless.

This time a flare did go up. Everyone froze and waited for it to go out. No machine gun fire eventuated, so the men went back to work. Another length of coiled barbed wire was placed on top of the first one. More were placed on top of the second one until the barbed wire stood above the heads of the men. With one hole mended, the lieutenant moved on to the next hole, and the whole process was repeated. The men worked throughout most of the night.

At one point a flare went up, which caught them tap-tap-tapping on a steel pike, and the Germans opened fire on their position. Two men were struck in the chest by the machine gun fire, while the others made it to the relative safety of the ground. Sergeant Williams and Lieutenant Bowen rolled into a shell hole and the others sought similar shelter elsewhere.

The German machine gun continued to pepper the ground around them—clack clack clack; followed by the odd rifle shots—bang bang. With so much gunfire being directed at their position, they were trapped where they were. When the German gunfire halted, the Australians didn't know what to do. If they moved, the gunfire might catch them in the open again, so they remained in their current position.

One of the Australians, who had been struck in the first volley of fire, was still alive and moaning from the pain of his injury. Unfortunately for the others, his cries were giving away their position. Lieutenant Bowen knew that something had to be done or they would be held here until daylight, and that would mean they would be here all of the next day.

Sergeant Williams and Lieutenant Bowen looked at each other.

'Things are not looking very good, Peter,' Sergeant Williams said. Having risen through the ranks together, Sergeant Williams and Lieutenant Bowen were on a first name basis whenever they were alone.

'Looks that way, Craig. The best we can hope for now is a break in the firing while we make a dash back to the lines.'

Just then, the Australian front line opened up on the German position. While this Australian fire poured into the Germans, Lieutenant Bowen and his squad were able to return to their trench. One man had been killed, another was badly wounded and needed evacuation. The remainder of the holes in the barbed wire would have to be fixed the next evening.

The soldier who had died was one of the newly arrived replacements from Australia. The men gathered around him and looked down on his lifeless body.

'If he was going to get killed over here,' Sergeant

Williams said, 'it was better that he got it now rather than suffer these trenches for months or even years before getting it. At least in this way he was lucky.'

Lieutenant Bowen nodded in agreement.

*　*　*

Sister Copley moved slowly through her ward of wounded Australian soldiers. She was in her early thirties but looked younger. She had long, blonde hair that was pulled back and tied up, with her sister's cap sitting in front. She had a charming smile and a warm greeting for all her patients, and they responded to her with a smile of their own. They called her their 'golden angel'.

She was married to a captain in the Royal Fusiliers, who was on active duty on the western front. She worried about Charles, especially when she saw the horrific wounds some of the Australians presented with. Each day, however, she pushed all thoughts of her husband from her mind and smiled sweetly as she moved among her patients. There were, of course, things that she checked daily with the nursing staff. The ward had to be spotless and the windows cleaned and opened for fresh air to circulate. The beds had to be freshly made and the patients cleaned, with their dressings renewed and their medications filled. Next, she would check the pantry and linen cupboards to see that they were clean and well stocked. Once her inspection was complete, she would accompany the doctors as they conducted their rounds.

Although Sister Ann Copley was English, she had been retained as a sister at the First Australian Auxiliary Hospital because she had been a founding member of the staff when the hospital opened in 1915. Her experience as a sister in a London hospital before she was married had helped her secure her initial position. She was happy with this arrangement because she preferred the down-to-earth approach of the Australians to her own country's class-structured way of doing things.

The First Australian Auxiliary Hospital was located at Harefield Park, Hillingdon, in the greater London area. It was a stately house that had been converted into a hospital, and was partially covered in ivy, which grew up the front and sides of the building. In places, the ivy was thick, especially near the windows, where it had been repeatedly cut back. The house had a gravel driveway and a small portico, which offered shelter for the patients, but not the vehicles which bought them to the hospital. There was a garage with two Crossley Tender motorised ambulances for transporting patients from the railway station or the docks to the hospital. The hospital also had a grassy outdoor area with large shady trees that afforded the playing of concerts, including solo piano performances as well as the more traditional vaudeville shows. Patients could be brought out on their beds, or seated in chairs, or even laid on the grassy slopes.

Harefield Hospital contained over one thousand beds for casualties from France, most of which were surgical and amputee cases. Ann tried to keep up-to-date with the latest treatment for her patients. The problem was that most of them presented with seriously infected wounds. The wounds themselves, if treated quickly and cleanly, would probably heal without much trouble— but they weren't treated quickly or cleanly. The trenches on the western front in France were far from clean, with mud, vermin and germs from decaying bodies being part of a soldier's everyday existence. Add to this the delay of days before adequate treatment was commenced and you had a recipe for tragedy.

The war had been going for two years now, yet most patients still had to have their limbs amputated or they would die from their wounds. Unfortunately, gangrene was a common sight in Ann's ward, and she was tired of its consequences—tired of the way it ruined the lives of thousands of young men. If only there were a way of treating these wounds properly before they presented at the hospital in England. But for now, that was only a wish, a desire in her for something better for her patients. Wishing, however, was futile.

Not long after the gaps in the wire had been plugged, Lieutenant Bowen's 9th Battalion was moved back from the front to Mametz, where the soldiers underwent hard training. They did three weeks of charging and bayonet practice on frozen ground. After that, they had a few days' rest at Shelter Wood, near Fricourt. They had hot baths in huge tubs that held up to twenty men at a time. They were given clean underwear and even had their uniforms steam cleaned in an attempt to rid them of lice. Such luxury after the mud of the trenches was an unexpected indulgence.

To top it all off, they were given leave to go into town. Lieutenant Bowen and Sergeant Williams went into town together. First, they stopped at the Red Cross and were given some woollen socks, which had been knitted by people back home. The socks were appreciated on the cold nights in the trenches. They were also given a hot cup of tea and some biscuits.

After that, they visited the Australian Comforts Fund, which was holding a vaudeville show. They sat for a while and watched some singers performing popular songs, some dancers, comedians and a juggler. They decided to leave after the juggler and make for the more popular estaminets.

On entering one shabby French café, they were greeted by confusion and mayhem. Some soldiers stood on the estaminet bar singing, *Waltzing Matilda*. Others were betting each other on who could climb up and down a staircase the fastest. This led to soldiers climbing up and falling down stairs at regular intervals. Some were also trying to get a few French women to perform a can-can, while other women circulated through the crowd offering their services for a price that most soldiers thought was too expensive.

Lieutenant Bowen thought it best if he did not stay, so he left Sergeant Williams in the estaminet for a quiet walk in the town. He had not walked far when a young woman approached him.

'Hello, soldier. You like me, no?'

'Oh, yes. Sure. You look great.'

'You come home with me, yes?'

Lieutenant Bowen reflected on the lectures he had been given about the evils of venereal disease, and how at the time they had little effect on him or his men. Most men on the front believed they were on borrowed time, so the possibility of getting a disease after they were dead was of little consequence to them. Now that he was confronted with this opportunity, he felt it hard to resist.

'No. No, thank you. I'm just looking around.'

'Sure, Chérie. You can look at me, no? It is my patriotic duty, no?'

'Gosh lady, you sure are persistent, I'll say that for you. But no, sorry.'

'Okay, Chérie. Maybe next time, yes?'

'Yes, maybe. Next time.'

He left her and spent the rest of his day walking around town and getting his picture taken so he could send a photo back home to his folks.

Ann arrived home late, because she had spent extra time reading about the new 'Carrel-Dakin' treatment of deep wounds, which used a large-bore gravity-fed antiseptic irrigation. Apparently, the crucial factor in the treatment was using the exact concentration of the Carrel-Dakin solution, which had to be precisely and reliably applied. If she were to use it in her ward, she would have to order the solution and ensure it was properly applied, and that would require the assistance and enthusiasm of the nursing staff and the doctors. She felt this would be best achieved if she were to show how successful it could be. What she needed was for the doctors to agree to order the solution, and for her to pick a soldier who presented with the right type of wound. She would have to be on the lookout for such a case, but she knew it would not be long before one presented itself in her ward. As for ordering the solution, she felt the doctors would allow her to order it if she explained how it worked. The Australians were open to innovation, especially if it helped in the treatment of wounds and might lead to the saving of a limb.

'Where have you been, Ann? Dinner was served a long time ago,' Joan, Ann's mother-in-law asked.

'Yes, I'm sorry, but I was working on something very important for my patients.'

'Why you bother so much about those colonials, I'll never know. Everyone knows how crude they are.'

Joan was quick to draw distinctions between the classes, believing herself to be among the better class. Ann herself felt that the reports about the Australians were exaggerated, and that they were a lot like any other group of people—some were good, some were mediocre and some were bad.

'Crude or not, they are dying for us and our cause.'

'Well, I suppose you are right about that. But why you persist in staying in their hospital, when you could be working in one of our own, I'll never know.'

'Perhaps I like working there. Perhaps I like their ways better than ours.'

'What do you mean by that?' It was said as more of an accusation than a question.

'Well, they are more down-to-earth. More concerned about how a job is done than the person who is doing it. You know I detest the class system, which is endemic in this country and holding us back.'

'That class system has created the greatest empire this world has ever known. You ought to remember that, my Dear.'

She said it with such triumph in her voice, it was used more as a statement of fact than an issue of debate, but Ann could not let it go. She knew that she was being stubborn by arguing with her mother-in-law, and would regret going too far, but she was tired and irritable and simply could not let such ignorance go unchallenged.

'What created that empire, was not the class system you so eagerly defend, but the entrepreneurial spirit, which created the largest industrial base of any country on earth. That is, until the Germans and Americans caught up to us. Now that has happened, our empire will simply fade away. That is what would have happened if this war had not interfered. Now I think the Americans will become even more powerful with all the money that we and the French owe them for their help in this war.'

'Well, I never! I can't believe you are so unpatriotic. England is the greatest country on earth, and we will beat Germany in this war and prove it.'

There she goes again, Ann thought, *defending something that was causing such a catastrophe on a global scale.* At times like this, Ann wondered if this was really a war between nations or simply the clash of pride between two classes—the English upper class and the German Junker class. Oh, that was a part of it but not the whole picture. She knew that but she wondered if the enormous losses suffered on the battlefield would be tolerated by any class other than the aristocracy of both countries, who were the ones leading and making the decisions. Oh, but she was so tired of going round and round when it came to the war and the classes; better just to live with it and do her job to the best of her ability and save as many lives as she could.

Before the war, Ann and Charles had a child born with a hole in its heart. The child lived for just ten days, during which time Ann breastfed it. She felt a great loss when the child died and had become depressed for many months after. At first, Charles tried to cheer her up, but when that didn't have any effect on her, he resumed his life and gradually withdrew from her. This made Ann feel that Charles was callous and seemingly oblivious to her suffering and the loss she was feeling, and she began to resent him for that. What she could not understand, nor forgive Charles for, was the way he could move on so easily after such a crushing event in their lives.

When the war broke out, Ann knew there would be many wives and mothers who would feel the same loss she felt, when they lost a loved one to the war. She decided to do something about it, and had become involved in hospital work, in order to alleviate their suffering. At first, this was welcomed by Ann's mother-in law. After all, she could boast about her caring daughter-in-law and her courageous hospital work.

When Ann joined the Australian hospital, however, Joan's attitude changed. It was difficult for her to boast about the work Ann was doing with those Australian ruffians. Ann admitted quietly to herself that she was pleased with this reaction and that made her more determined to stay at the Australian hospital.

On this night, however, she had had enough with the circumlocution between herself and Joan. She was tired and hungry, and carrying on this conversation seemed pointless.

'I'm sorry. Can we just end this for now? I have a lot

of work to do tomorrow, so I hope you will forgive me and let me have my dinner and go to bed.'

'Yes, of course, Dear.'

And there it ended once again. Nothing resolved, nothing gained on either side. Just another pointless argument between two entrenched viewpoints. Ann longed for some resolution, some coming together, but this seemed endless and she wondered where it would lead.

* * *

After the men had returned to the front following their three-day rest, they were told that there would be another 'big push'. Word finally came through to Lieutenant Bowen that the jump-off time for the attack at Messines was to be 12:00 noon that day. He passed word to the rest of the company.

This was the time most men dreaded—the waiting. A young soldier's face turned a green-yellow colour as he dry-retched into the trench. The rest pushed their bodies into the mud of the trench wall, their fresh clean uniforms already soiled in layers of mud.

Some tanks appeared behind the battalion and moved through the troops. Each tank had a man walking several metres in front to guide it. He held a flag in each hand and would guide the tank driver by raising one arm, which was a signal for the driver to steer the tank to the right or left, depending on which arm was raised. With the visibility of the tank driver being restricted to his immediate front, such a move was necessary, but it made a target of the man carrying the flags. German snipers could pick him off, then the tank would wander over the battlefield causing disruption for the troops.

This was followed by the arrival of horse-drawn cannons. The horses were detached, and as the cannons were turned to face the enemy, the horses, led by their handlers, dashed to the rear to bring up more cannons.

Suddenly, the cannons began firing. The noise was deafening, and the soldiers in the trench pushed themselves further into the mud, dreading the order to launch the attack. Now that the cannons had started firing, the enemy was sure to know that an attack was imminent, and they would focus their cannons and machine guns accordingly.

It was 11:30 am, just half an hour before jump-off time. An order came through for the 9th to put on their respirators. There was a sense of urgency as they all scrambled to get out their respirators and fit them to their faces, making sure that the rubber flaps fitted correctly. An air-tight seal was essential if the respirators were to be of any use. However, this made the soldiers' breathing harder and the eyeglasses began to fog up, but they were soon grateful for the order as gas explosions began dropping around them. Lieutenant Bowen was thankful for the gas, as it would offer his troops some camouflage during the attack.

Suddenly, tremendous explosions erupted under the German lines as the explosives, put there by the tunnelling of conscripted miners, blew gaping holes in the earth. The explosions were so great that windows rattled in London.

At 11:55 am, with just five minutes to go, Lieutenant Bowen issued an order to fix bayonets and load a live round into the firing chamber. This order was carried out quickly and quietly, each man going over in his mind his final thoughts before having to go over the top. *Will he survive this attack? Will he ever see his family again? Will it hurt if he gets hit?* Such thoughts almost paralysed the troops, but they all knew that when the whistle blew, they would rise over the trench and start their perilous dash to the enemy's trenches.

The whistle was blown, the men went over, and

already some of them were dropping. The big tanks lumbered slowly towards Messines Ridge. The troops following them adopted an artillery formation, in little groups of six or eight, one man behind the other. These groups moved inexorably towards the German trenches.

The English and Australian cannons set up a creeping barrage. Every three minutes, the barrage was lifted a hundred metres. The flash and burst of the big guns could be heard as a dull sobbing in England, but to the advancing troops it was close enough and loud enough to send shudders through their bodies.

The German guns began to find their range. Now, enemy shells were landing among the advancing troops. They went to ground and rose again to push on some more, only to go to ground again and repeat the pattern over and over. As they got closer to their objectives, more and more men dropped or disappeared in shell bursts.

Finally, they reached the German line to discover dozens of broken, smashed trenches. Dead Germans could be seen in their hundreds. In one place there was a huge hole in the ground, over one hundred metres in diameter and up to thirty-five metres deep. Such destruction would make it impossible to determine who died here; so many Germans had been blown apart or buried. They would be reported to their loved ones as 'missing in action, presumed dead'.

Still the Australians had to keep going, as they needed to establish a new line 250 metres further on. The German cannon fire was still falling among them, but the German soldiers seemed to be further away, and had not yet taken up positions to oppose them.

They reached their objective and began to stretch a white tape to mark their line. This was done to assist the fresh troops following them to establish their line of advance, before setting off on their own journey into hell. The tape was, however, a double-edged weapon, as it clearly marked a target for the German artillery. That was why it was so important for the fresh troops to be at their starting point quickly, but that was not the case. They were still coming up the hill towards the 9th, who were digging in as fast as they could to establish a new support line and get cover from the German artillery. The battalion took an awful pounding from the Germans over the next ten minutes, before the fresh companies moved through their line and began making their own advance.

It was at this point that a German shell burst close to Lieutenant Bowen's position, and he was blown into the air. As he cartwheeled to the ground, he felt a searing pain in his right thigh. Dizziness enveloped him and he had trouble making out what was going on around him. A wave of darkness engulfed him; then he slipped into unconsciousness.

* * *

Charles Copley had been promoted to captain and transferred to GHQ in 1916, when his battalion had been disbanded. The battle of Messines Ridge had been brilliantly planned and executed. The men had achieved their objectives, with the ridge south of Ypres captured. Now, those planning the British strategy believed they could finally breakout in an attack against Passchendaele by using the lessons learned from Messines. However, that would take a lot of planning and preparation. The British High Command had renewed hope in making the Ypres offensive a decisive one and putting an end to the carnage that had overtaken both armies.

In the past, each time a bulge had been achieved in either side's line, a breakout had not followed, and this left the attacking force's flanks vulnerable to counterattack. In the end, this left little achieved except for a few hundred metres of land and tens, if not hundreds, of thousands dead or wounded. This time, however, the British were hopeful of achieving the breakout necessary to drive the Germans out of the coastal region and the surrender of their submarine bases in Holland, resulting in such a major setback for the Germans that they might want to sue for peace.

This was the official perspective of the British High Command, but some of the junior officers were critical of yet another 'big push', when they had all failed in the past. The junior officers preferred a 'small bite' approach, which would not lead to high casualties. Charles favoured the 'big push' approach and believed in Field Marshal Haig's war of attrition. Sooner or later, he believed, the Germans would lose their will to win, and their home front would collapse. What this approach did not take into account, however, was the effect it would have on their own soldiers and their own home front.

'The field marshal himself is coming today. I want everyone to be on high alert and to answer any of his questions in positive and decisive terms,' Major Chatsworth, Charles' commanding officer, said to his assembled staff. 'After he has carried out his inspection, just go about your normal work, but be prepared to answer any of his questions.'

Major Chatsworth looked around at his staff for signs that the significance of his words had sunk in. Then, he told them to gather outside on the steps of their headquarters for inspection.

When Field Marshal Haig arrived in his shiny new Rolls Royce, Major Chatsworth brought his staff to attention and met with the general as he alighted from his vehicle. After the inspection, they went inside, where Field Marshal Haig addressed them all.

'Gentlemen, we will mount another major attack along the Ypres salient. We will build upon the success of Messines Ridge, which has demoralised our enemy. If we are successful, we will shatter our enemy's entire northern defences and deprive the Germans of their will to win. This could be the battle that ends this war, gentlemen, and I expect each of you to do a thorough job of our preparations for a successful outcome.' Haig's tired eyes surveyed his staff once more. 'England is counting on you, lads. Let's not let her down.'

Then he was gone, and the staff members all stood looking at one another. Finally, one of them spoke up.

'Just what England needs right now. Another big push.'

'You heard the field marshal,' Charles said. 'This will be decisive. We have to make this one count.'

'Just like all the others, Charles? After two years of big pushes, what makes you think this one will end in any other way than the ones before it?'

'You all need to believe in Field Marshal Haig's strategy for success. Why can't you see that this one will change the war for us?'

'Charles, can't you see that despite the appalling loss of life, all Field Marshal Haig has called for is yet another big push, which will end like all the others? A huge number of deaths and casualties will be all we will have to show for it. Can't you see that this war has become little more than an extended game of attack and counterattack with little to show for it than a tremendous loss of life?'

'What I see is someone whose talk is sapping our will to fight. You really can't hold that view and continue fighting.'

'Yes, I can. I just want a change in strategy. Can't you see that the current one is not working? If we just took small bites and then consolidated, we could then inflict heavy casualties on the enemy when they try to counterattack.'

'Such nonsense,' Charles said. 'Don't you think Field Marshal Haig has thought of that? Obviously, that won't work. Otherwise, he would have tried it.'

Those with Charles felt embarrassed by his chauvinistic optimism, so they left him alone with Major Chatsworth and retreated to their desks.

'We can't make any mistakes with this one, Major. It could be decisive. It could make a difference this time,' Charles said.

'I hope you're right, son. I don't know how much longer our country can be depended on to continue making such heavy sacrifices,' Major Chatsworth said.

'Oh, don't worry, Sir. We will prevail. We always do. It would be a pity to throw it in now—now that we have come so far.'

'Yes, yes. A pity indeed.'

* * *

Not long after Field Marshal Haig's visit, Charles was given a four-day leave pass to refresh his mind before commencing preparations for the Ypres 'big push'. Charles had wanted to get started right away on the preparations, but his CO insisted he take a break, so he took a train into the Gare du Nord railway station in Paris, and from there he walked to the Rue la Fayette where he checked into a small hotel. Charles had already done enough of the Paris sightseeing that he wanted to do, so this time he was determined to enjoy himself and that was why he had checked into a relatively small and unknown hotel, where there were no other British officers.

That night he took his dinner in the small restaurant of his hotel. His meal was simple—steak and vegetables. He had missed the clean, simple meals of home, and was not swayed by the delicate French cuisine offered by the hotel. For a moment during his meal he thought about his wife, but quickly pushed her out of his mind because he had not invited her to join him in Paris and he did not want thoughts of her spoiling this time he had set aside for himself. Ever since the death of their child, Ann had become withdrawn and unwilling to try and make a go of their marriage. To his mind, Charles did not want Ann here to spoil the fun time he hoped to enjoy on his leave. He had even become annoyed at his wife's attitude of late. He felt that her letters to him spoke more and more about her work at the hospital and less and less about her affection for him. *Besides*, he told himself, *Ann would find it hard to get to Paris and would probably prefer to stay in England with her patients.*

After his meal, Charles took the Metro to Blanche Station in the Montmartre district of Paris. He walked the streets towards the Moulin Rouge, where he hoped to take in the cabaret and get drunk.

'Bonjour, Monsieur.'

Charles turned to see a very attractive young woman, who moved up closer to him. She had an ivory complexion, long black hair, blue eyes and a slim waist. But what really caught his attention was her smile, which showed her teeth and curled the corners of her mouth, producing two cute dimples in her cheeks.

'Bonjour … er … is it Madame or Mademoiselle?'

'What would you like it to be, Monsieur?'

'Tonight, it really doesn't matter to me.'

'Then let us leave it at that. Why don't you just call me Yvette, which is my name. Would you like me to join you tonight and help you celebrate?'

'Yes, of course. Please do, Yvette.'

They walked to the Moulin Rouge. When she discovered where he was taking her, she slipped her arm through his and held him tight.

When they were seated in the cabaret room, Charles

ordered champagne, then turned to Yvette and said, 'I have already eaten, my Dear, but would *you* like something to eat?'

'Oh, yes. Please.'

Charles thought she looked like she had gone without adequate food for at least two weeks. She seemed almost too eager in her response.

Charles ordered beef bourguignon pot pie with celeriac mash for Yvette, and baked croissants with cherry custard for both of them. Charles believed that his guests should eat what he ordered for them, so they could judge his taste, good or otherwise. They drank the champagne and ate in silence. Yvette ate slowly, taking small pieces into her mouth and chewing deliberately, in an apparent attempt to hide her hunger.

'Are you married, Yvette?' Charles asked.

'I thought that didn't matter?'

'I changed my mind. I am more interested in you now.'

'Oh, I see. Well, yes. I am married to a Parisian, who was sent to the front. I haven't heard from him in three months. The French government has him listed as 'missing in action, presumed dead'.'

Charles knew what that meant. They could not find

his body. So many young men went that way, usually from being blown to pieces by artillery fire.

'Oh, I am sorry, Yvette.' Charles could see that she had come to terms with the loss of her husband, but that there was something else in her demeanour, something almost desperate. He let it pass and went on as though he had not noticed.

'And do you have any children?'

'No, no children. We were only married for a short time before he was deployed. No, I have no one. Just myself. As you see me.'

'And you look lovely, Yvette. Truly lovely.'

She looked like she was trying to hold back tears at hearing this, however, she caught herself and smiled broadly.

'Why,' she said, 'I do believe you are flirting with me.'

'Oh yes, my Dear. Indeed I am. And may I introduce myself? My name is Charles Copley.'

'Pleased to meet you, Charles Copley,' Yvette replied with a broad smile on her face. Then they both laughed and enjoyed the rest of their meal in quiet contemplation of what was to come.

The cabaret was the usual wonderful dance and comedy routine that the Moulin Rouge had become famous for. The can-can was performed by tall, well-proportioned female dancers, who moved with high-stepping cheerfulness across the stage and out into the front tables.

As the night wore on, Charles became increasingly excited. The alcohol was beginning to take effect. Charles was the type of man who allowed alcohol to sexually arouse him. He began flirting with the waitresses and put his hand on Yvette's knee. Whenever he looked at her, Yvette smiled back and moved her head closer to his. Charles liked this and responded by smiling back and moving his hand a little higher on her thigh.

When Charles was ready to leave, he asked Yvette whether she wanted to return to his hotel with him.

'Yes, of course, Dear. I have nowhere else to go,' she replied.

Charles smiled and led the way back to the Metro. Arriving at the hotel, they immediately took the iron-gated lift to Charles' floor.

Charles let Yvette enter the room ahead of him, and as he entered he kicked the door closed with his foot. Yvette turned to face him and he took her in his arms and kissed her hard. His hand found its way to the inside of her thigh. Then he picked her up and carried her to his bed, where he took her without any pretence at romance.

It was over quickly. Immediately, he rose from her and went to the hand basin to wash himself down. When he returned to the bed, Yvette was still lying on her back. She held up her arms to greet him and welcomed him back to her side. The rest of the night was spent in broken bouts of sleep and physical contact.

In the morning, Charles invited Yvette to breakfast. He ordered bacon and eggs with hot coffee, while Yvette had a croissant with hot black coffee. She placed dark chocolate on her tongue and drank the coffee over it. The chocolate melted and offered a sweetener for the bitter black coffee.

When they had finished their breakfast, Charles turned to Yvette. He had intended to end their association that morning, but something held him back. Perhaps it was the desire for another night with her. Perhaps it was the beauty of her face, the deep blue of her eyes, or the longing he saw there for more than what they had just shared. He knew she was desperate for something more than what her current life offered her, so Charles decided not to end their affair that morning.

'I want to go to the Eiffel Tower today. Would you like

to join me?' Charles asked. Although he had intended not to do any sightseeing of Paris on this trip, he found himself wanting to do it with Yvette. He liked the idea of being seen with her.

'Oh, yes. I would love to spend the day with you, Charles. I like you a lot, you see, and would enjoy any time you can give me.'

With those words ringing in his ears, Charles' face lit up, and he took Yvette's hand and squeezed it.
The next three days saw them do all the things Charles had told himself he would not do. They went to the Eiffel Tower and took the elevator to the top where they looked at Paris laid out before them. They walked the Champs-Élysées and took coffee in a quaint sidewalk café. They stood under the Arch de Triomphe. They took in the great works of art at the Louvre. Standing in front of the Mona Lisa, they wondered at the mystery of her smile and the mountain road that wound its way behind her.

Finally, on their last day together, they went to the Cathédrale de Notre-Dame. Yvette knelt in a back pew and prayed. Charles was mystified as to how she could do that with what had happened between them over the past few days, but he said nothing.

In the end, the time came for them to say goodbye. Tears welled in Yvette's eyes and she did her best to stem their flow. Charles knew that the thought of being alone again, on the cold streets of Paris, filled her with dreaded anticipation.

They stood on the platform of the Gare du Nord, while Charles waited to board the steaming train. He looked down on Yvette's upturned face and saw the despair in her eyes. Suddenly, he realised this could be the last time he would see her, and that thought made him desperate—something he had not felt since his estrangement from Ann, and that seemed such a long time ago. He realised he wanted to go on seeing Yvette, so he took her hands and smiled at her.

He gave her money to get herself set up in some kind of lodgings, and he also gave her his postal address.

'Write me when you are settled and I will send you more money for food,' Charles said.

'Oh Charles, I have prayed for us to be together beyond this day. Thank you, Darling.' The tears she had been holding back suddenly broke and she wept openly and fell into his arms. They kissed, and Charles felt a surge of emotion that made him want to stay with her, but he knew he had to return to his unit. He clung desperately to her until they finally broke from their embrace. Then Charles boarded the train as it pulled away from the platform. Yvette stood waving until the train disappeared down the track before turning and walking away, with a smile on her face.

When the artillery shell had landed near Peter Bowen and had blown him into the air, a large piece of shrapnel had cut a deep wound through his right thigh and driven him into unconsciousness. The soil that had been blown into Peter's wound was relatively clean dirt, as opposed to the bacteria-ridden soil of no-man's land, and this contributed to the slower development of gangrene—something that was to be significant when Peter eventually arrived at Ann's hospital in England.

Two stretcher bearers had taken Peter from the battlefield to the nearest field ambulance. They took one look at his wound and sent him to a casualty clearing station, where his clothes were cut away and his wound was cleaned and dressed. Then he was given back his cut uniform and some pins to hold it together.

Peter was then put into an ambulance and transported

to the nearest railway station. From there, he was transported by rail to the closest port for evacuation to England. By the time Peter arrived in Ann Copley's Ward, he had had his wound cleaned and dressed three times. It had been six days since he was wounded, but luckily, gangrene had not yet set in. This was the exact wound Ann had been waiting for. Ann looked down on Peter, who was still lying on the stretcher he had come into the hospital on.

Peter looked young and strong and this helped Ann to make up her mind. She told Peter what she wanted to do with his leg and the possible risk he would face. She explained that what she proposed could save his leg, but that if gangrene set in he would lose his leg and possibly even his life. Peter agreed with her that he wanted to try anything to save his leg from amputation. Whatever the risk, he had said, he wanted to save his leg.

Ann noticed his piercing blue eyes, his courage and his earnest, intelligent expression, and she was moved. Shaking slightly from the intensity of the moment, her heart skipped a beat. Ann smiled down at Peter, who smiled back at her.

Ann left Peter and immediately went to the chief

surgeon, who was scheduled to amputate Peter's leg that afternoon.

'I would like to try and save this soldier's leg,' she said.

'I know you have been keen to try that new method on a patient, Sister Copley, but what makes you think this is the right patient? His wound is very deep and it is now an old wound.'

'Yes, Doctor, but there is only a little infection in the wound, which you can easily remove. Surely, it is worth a try?'

'Well, if we succeed it will be, but if we fail, it could cost this boy his life. Remember, his wound is close to his hip which doesn't leave me much to work with if the infection continues after the operation. Is he prepared to take that risk, and are you prepared to take that risk, Sister?'

'Yes, Doctor. He is, and I am confident we can save his leg.'

There was something about the clarity of Ann's words that led the surgeon to believe she would take personal charge of this patient.

'You realise you will be held responsible for this patient's recovery, Sister?'

'Yes, Doctor.' Ann's voice held her conviction and her confidence in this new venture.

'All right then. I'll operate on him and put in the irrigation shunt. The rest is up to you, Sister.'

'Thank you, Doctor.'

* * *

It took Charles two weeks to get his next leave pass, and during that time he could not get Yvette out of his mind. He knew he needed to concentrate more on his work, to make sure he identified where the Germans had hidden their artillery, but often he would find himself reliving in his mind his time with Yvette. He often wondered how effective he was at his job, but he pushed those thoughts aside and just ploughed on, concentrating as best he could on the job at hand.

The Germans, on the other hand, had become expert at camouflaging their artillery, making it much harder to identify them from the aerial photographs taken by the high-flying photographic planes. If the planes flew any lower, however, it exposed them to ground attack, and the Germans had increased their aerial activity over the Ypres Salient following the Allied success at Messines Ridge. This often exposed the British reconnaissance planes to attack from the air, making such sorties very dangerous. Sensing another attack in this area, the Germans had intensified their defensive positions, bringing men and equipment from other areas of their line. If an attack were to come, they would be ready for it.

None of this mattered to Charles, who took some more leave so he could be with Yvette. When he arrived in Paris, Charles went straight to Yvette's apartment. She greeted him at the door and they immediately embraced. He kissed her long and hard and she responded by wrapping her arms around him and holding him tightly to her.

This time, they took their breakfast in a nearby sidewalk café, after which they took a long walk in the park opposite. They followed this routine each day and on one of these walks they sat quietly on a park bench. Charles seemed preoccupied with something, so Yvette left him to his thoughts. Eventually, Charles turned to her and engaged her eyes.

'I love you, Yvette,' he said.

It had come out so suddenly and so simply. He seemed to have no power over what he said. He only knew it had to be said and he was glad it was finally out. For a fleeting moment he had thought about his wife, but he had quickly put her aside. He knew he should not be talking to another woman like this while he was married to Ann, but that did not seem to matter to him now. He had already left his love for Ann far behind. Besides, he told himself, Yvette knew he was married before they had started their affair. So he felt, at least in this way, they were both compliant in their actions.

'I think about you all the time. You are never out of my mind,' he said.

'Oh, Charles. How wonderful. It is the same for me, *Mon Amour*. I just keep wanting you to be with me,' she said.

They went quiet after that—neither of them wanting to break the magic of the moment, nor to raise the subject that had to be raised. At first, Charles began with small talk about Paris, and asked Yvette how she felt about living here. Yvette responded with her own small talk about how she liked her current circumstances and filled Charles in with the details of her life in Paris. Finally, Charles took her hands in his.

'Would you like to go back to the apartment now?' he asked.

'Of course, Darling. This is your time. Whatever you want I am willing to give you,' she replied.

They went back to Yvette's apartment, which was a

small, modest three-room dwelling to the east of the Sorbonne. They immediately went to the bedroom and stayed there all afternoon, waking on occasions to make love and then returning to their slumber. It was a wonderful, luxurious time for both of them. Occasionally, Charles would stand, walk to the window and look out on the cold tiled roofs of the buildings beside them. He was happy to be here with Yvette and to shut out the rest of the world. He smiled at her frequently and whispered his thanks to her, and she would return his smile and kiss him lightly on his cheeks and lips.

'Oh, Chérie,' she would whisper back, 'how happy you have made me. Now I have a reason to go on living. You have given me so much, my Darling.'

It was at one of these moments that Charles, unable to contain his love for her any longer, broached the forbidden topic.

'Yvette, you know that I am married …' he began.

'Shhh, my Darling. I keep telling myself that you are married, but it makes no difference to me. I love you and we are together now. Can we make that be enough?' she asked.

'I must explain, Yvette. What we have shared together

these last few days transcends my marriage. I feel you have opened up a new potential for me—a potential for a better life. I want you to be with me always, Yvette.'

'Oh, Charles. How wonderful.'

'Yes, I know, and I want it now more than ever.'

Charles then went on to explain how his marriage to Ann had stalled and declined since the death of their child over a year ago and how Ann now seemed more interested in her patients at the hospital than in him. When Charles had finished, Yvette smiled and squeezed his hands.

'Oh, Charles. My poor Dear,' she said. 'It is not for me to judge, for I am a woman in love, and I want you so desperately.'

'Yes, that is my point exactly. This war will not go on forever. What will become of us when it ends is something that I must prepare for now. I don't want to lose you, Yvette. Not now. Now that you mean so much to me.'

'I too, do not want to lose you, Charles. But why worry about that now? The war is still far from decided. Can't we just go on like this until the end is near?'

'The end may be nearer than you think, and I want something in place before it does end.'

'But Charles, what do you want from me? I am willing

to give you whatever you want. Just tell me what you want.'

'What if I separated from Ann and was free?'

'If you are asking me if I would live with you if the war were over and if you were separated from Ann, then I would agree. Only, you must recognise there are a lot of 'ifs' in that equation—'ifs' that must first be resolved. First, the war has to end, and second, you have to separate from your wife. Why don't we just leave it until those issues are resolved?'

'Yes, I see that, Yvette, but I could write to Ann and tell her that I want to separate. At least I could do that now and be a little more prepared. At least that would work towards one resolution for us.'

'Yes, Darling. You could do that. Would you do that for me?'

'Oh, yes. In a heartbeat. You mean so much to me, Yvette.'

They enjoyed the rest of Charles' leave together. They were never apart from each other for the whole time of his brief leave, and Charles' fascination for Yvette grew with every passing day. He saw them being like this for the rest of their lives, and that thought cheered his spirits.

Yvette too had been thinking about Charles' wife, but she also had pushed Ann from her mind. She remembered how lonely the streets of Paris had been after she had run out of money; how hungry and desperate she had become, and how she hated the cold hands and the stinking breath of the one-night stands she had been forced into to keep herself alive. Now that she had Charles' love, she was determined not to go back to the streets. No. Any thoughts of Ann had to be reconciled with the cold hard facts of her circumstances, and when thought of in this way, Ann became second by a long margin. Besides, she told herself, she too loved Charles in her own way. He had been so kind to her. True, he had cheated on his wife, and as he explained the decline of his marriage to her, Yvette had begun to form a more favourable picture of Ann in her mind. She also began, for the first time, to see Charles as more selfish than she had imagined he could be. However, she said nothing of her doubts at that time. For now, she would be happy with whatever Charles was willing to give her.

CHAPTER 5

Sometime after the attack on Messines Ridge and Peter's evacuation, Sergeant Williams was promoted to lieutenant, which placed him in charge of the platoon. They had dug in at their designated line, and when the other battalions had passed through them to advance further into German territory, they went from being in the front line to the support line to the reserve line.

What followed was a German counterattack, which was halted by the front-line defenders, so Lieutenant Williams and his platoon were not involved. They were all grateful for the courageous and determined resistance of their front-line soldiers in holding the Germans, and not having to be involved themselves. They were well aware of the kind of sacrifice such resistance involved, and all were proud of the success they had achieved at Messines Ridge.

Lieutenant Williams and his platoon held their positions for the next three weeks before they were relieved and sent to the rear for further training and rest. Their training included more bayonet and target practice, and some of the platoon were sent for bomb training. The new Mills hand bomb had been invented in 1915, specifically for trench clearance, and a competent thrower could manage a throw of up to fifteen metres. The bomb did, however, have a lethal range greater than this, so the thrower had to take shelter after throwing. Consequently, the bomb was fitted with a seven-second fuse. This bomb would later become known as a hand grenade, which, when it exploded, shattered into fragments, tearing into many troops occupying the confined space of a trench. Of course, this training meant that Lieutenant Williams' platoon would be used for trench clearance in the next 'big push'. Although they were happy to use any new weapon that would help them do their job, they did not relish the relatively dangerous job of trench clearance, which inevitably involved bloody, hand-to-hand combat, and left many men mentally scarred for life.

It was during a morning tea break in their training when Lieutenant Williams was sitting with his new sergeant, that he first noticed a slight tremor in his left hand. He tried to control it, but it seemed to have a will of its own. He held it with his right hand until the tremor settled and subsided.

The new platoon sergeant, Sergeant Jones, had transferred in from a battalion that had been disbanded, owing to a lack of sufficient volunteers from Australia to make up for its casualty-depleted numbers. What the commanders decided to do was to bring the surviving battalions to full strength by disbanding some depleted battalions. It was a move that the members of the disbanded battalions disliked. Some members of those battalions showed their displeasure by striking. Of course, the army had no concept of striking soldiers—they called it mutiny. Eventually, however, these battalions were broken up, and their members transferred into other existing battalions.

'How do you think the men are going, Sergeant?' Lieutenant Williams asked his new confidant.

'They are as good as any other Australians, Sir.'

Lieutenant Williams was pleased to hear Sergeant Jones say that; it meant he was adjusting well. Lieutenant Williams had stayed out of his way and tried to distance himself from the platoon to allow Sergeant Jones a fair go at adjusting to his new position with the men. He had to admit to himself, however, that he missed the interaction with his men that he would otherwise have had.

'That's good, Frank. That's good. I'm glad you are settling in to your new position so well.'

'Yes, Sir. It has been hard, but the quicker the men accept me, and I fit in with them, the better we will all be.'

'Yes. If you need anything from me just let me know.'

'Well, Sir, things have gone smoothly so far. I don't think I'll be troubling you anytime soon.'

'Good. I'm pleased to hear that.'

They drifted into silence, and Lieutenant Williams found himself alone with his thoughts. He found it hard to control his thoughts now. Whenever he was left with time to reflect, his mind always went to the same images of the eyes of dying men. It was the eyes that never left him. There was a moment when those eyes went from being alive, with the light of life in them, to a glassy stare devoid of light; and it was to this moment that his mind ceaselessly returned. It haunted him with an intensity that he could not shake. He tried to think of more happy moments, from home and loved ones, but those glassy eyes kept coming back—over and over again.

Lieutenant Williams' left hand began shaking again, so he grabbed it with his right hand and squeezed it tightly.

'Are you all right, Lieutenant?' Sergeant Jones asked.

'Yes, Frank. I can control this. Don't worry, I won't let it affect my leadership of this platoon.'

'Yes, Sir. I am glad you are here. I wouldn't want to be leading the men by myself, and I know how much they look up to you. I want to help you in any way I can.'

'Thank you for that, but I'm fine, really.'

'Yes, Sir.'

He turned back to the men.

'All right, boys,' Sergeant Jones shouted, 'tea break is over! Let's get some practice on how to kill Germans. The more we kill, the quicker we get home.'

The men came to their feet with smiles on their faces. They had warmed to their new sergeant and his straight-and-direct orders. There was never any doubt about what he wanted his platoon to do.

* * *

Ann sat beside Peter's bed and was vigilant in checking and maintaining the correct flow of antiseptic irrigation fluid into his leg wound. She had held this bedside vigil for the last seven days and had not been home at all during that time. She had slept at the hospital so she could be near at hand in case anything went wrong. As it was, she had been putting in double shifts and had spent most of her time beside Peter's bed. Peter was aware of Ann's sacrifice and his admiration for her grew daily.

One day, when Peter was awake and looking out the window beside his bed, Ann came in and sat down next to him.

'How are you today, Lieutenant?' she asked.

'I'm fine thanks, but please call me Peter. I think we have known each other for a while now, and you have put so much time and effort into me.'

'Umm … well, only if you call me Ann.'

Ann knew that it was not proper for her to become too familiar with her patients, but Peter seemed different from the others. The truth was that she had felt very close to him over the past seven days. She had often sat beside him during the lonely nights and admired his physical features. Peter was over 180 cm, with a slim athletic build, dark brown hair and brown eyes. He was probably a little underweight, but Ann put that down to the poor diet of the trenches. He had a scar running across his forehead from an old wound. It had healed and was already beginning to fade. Whenever she had found herself thinking of Peter like this, however, she had reminded herself that she was married to Charles. Regardless of how their marriage was going, she knew she would remain faithful to him.

'Yes. Righto, Ann.'

Peter smiled up at her, waiting for her to continue.

'Well, the doctors are very pleased with your progress.'

'Yes. Well, I reckon that's all because of you.'

Ann smiled back down on Peter. It was always so comforting to know that her patients appreciated what she did for them.

'Thank you. You know, I have become something of a celebrity around here. The doctors all think I'm one in a million. Ha ha. But it took the two of us, you had to do your bit too. Now the doctors want to transfer you out of intensive care and put you into the surgical ward. How do you feel about that?'

'If they say so, I'm happy.'

'All right then, I'll arrange for the transfer.'

Peter reached out and held Ann's arm, as if a thought had just come to his mind.

'Just a minute, Ann. Will I still be seeing you?'

'Oh yes, I will come and see you once a day.'

'Oh … only once a day. Well maybe I should stay here a bit longer—it would be better to be sure.'

Ann looked into Peter's eyes and saw that he too had developed an attachment for her, and now he was reluctant to let go. This worried her briefly, but she had to do what was best for her patients. She knew that the hospital was quiet at the moment, since the battle had ended, and most of the patients had moved on to their rest centres before redeployment, so it would not hurt to have Peter stay a little longer.

Then, she remembered the nights she had spent with Peter. How she had sat beside him and imagined them as lovers. He was the kind of man she admired—the strong cheerful type, capable of saying the things that needed to be said but also with a cheerful disposition. She would look down on him and watch him stir occasionally. Sometimes he would jump and call out, 'No!' But he never woke up, and her feelings for him had become more personal than any she had ever had for anyone else, except her husband.

On these occasions she would remember how bad her marriage had become and she wondered what would become of her and Charles, and what Charles was doing while they were so far apart. Then she would feel guilty, because she thought of him as doing his duty. She thought of the suffering he must be going through. Her private thoughts tormented her, so she tried to shut them out of her mind. She knew Charles was overseas fighting for his country, and she would not become one of those fickle wives who had a good time while their husbands were away. Still, she had a responsibility to her patients and their welfare was foremost in her mind. The situation with Peter had developed through no fault of his, and she would have to be gentle with him for the sake of his recovery.

'All right then, I'll arrange with the doctor to keep you here for a couple more days before transferring you,' she said.

'Thank you, Ann. You are a swell girl.'

'And you are a swell bloke, Peter,' she said, smiling down on him. Then she took Peter's arm and laid it beside him, stood up, turned and left the room.

Peter was left wondering what would happen now. He could not believe he had said 'swell girl'! Such a stupid thing to say, and he hoped Ann had not taken it the wrong way. After all, he had wanted to compliment her, and that was the first thing that had come into his mind.

He realised he need not have worried, however, because Ann had smiled back at him before taking her leave.

He wanted so much to continue seeing Ann, even after he left the hospital, but he didn't see how that could be possible. Once he was well enough, he knew he would be transferred back to France. What was he going to do? How could he tell Ann how he felt about her when he knew she was married to a soldier fighting overseas? He sighed and turned back to look out the window once again.

The Third Battle of Ypres got underway on the last day of July and lasted until November, 1917. Field Marshal Sir Douglas Haig envisioned his attack sweeping across the low plains and swinging north to the sea. During the attack, millions of cannon shells exploded on the territory of both sides, turning the land into a cratered moonscape. On the first day of the attack, the British drove the Germans back because the Germans had adopted a scheme of defence in depth, consisting of a thinly-defended front line but a more strongly-defended support line. This was intended to slow the British advance and wear it down until it stopped. It was the tactic the German army had adopted after Messines Ridge.

'We have them now,' Charles pointed out to his fellow officers at Headquarters. 'This war will soon be over.'

'If the Germans continue to retreat, we will have the victory we have hoped for, but if they hold us on the low plains, we could be in for a terrible time,' a young captain in GHQ replied.

'Are you crazy? Our cannons, troops and tanks are crashing through their defences.'

'Yes, but the Germans still hold the high ground.'

'And that will fall in the next few days.'

'For all our sakes, I hope you are right, Charles.'

'Oh, I'm right. Field Marshall Haig will have his victory in the next few days and prove all his naysayers wrong.'

They went quiet after that, and Charles retreated to the privacy of his desk. He took out a writing pad and began writing a letter to Ann, telling her of his plans to separate from her. Now that the war was coming to an end, he wanted to go to Yvette and propose something concrete to her, but to do that, he knew he had to settle things with Ann first.

Like all things Charles did, his letter was short and to the point. He simply told Ann of his plan to separate from her, pointing out that their lives had taken different paths. He did not mention Yvette, preferring to keep that secret to himself.

Over the next few days, it rained the worst it had in seventy-five years, turning the whole battlefield into a quagmire. This stalled the British attack until August 10th. When it restarted, the soldiers and the tanks had become bogged down in the mud and were easy targets for the German artillery and machine guns. By late September, it had become apparent that the Allies would not achieve the great victory that Haig had expected but, undaunted, he ordered his troops to continue the attack.

'This is nonsense,' a junior officer in the British High Command commented. 'We are wasting the lives of thousands of our troops.'

'Yes, but we must push on to ultimate victory,' Charles replied. 'The Germans can't take much more of this, and when they crack the war will be over, and that will save the lives of those who would have to fight in a new battle later on.'

'But they are not going to crack. If they were going to, it would have happened by now. All we are doing now is wasting more lives in a lost cause.'

'That can't be true. We are still taking ground.'

'A few metres here and there, but then they counterattack and the line just swings backward and forward with neither side gaining the upper hand.'

'I don't believe that. The Germans are weakening and now we are going to use the Australians and Canadians. Fresh troops against tired German troops. We have more men at our disposal than they have.'

'What a terrible way to win a war, Charles. Just keep killing until one side runs out of men.'

'I thought that was how all wars were fought.'

'No, Charles. Only this terrible war of attrition talks about 'total war' and 'ultimate victory'. Anyway, had we stopped advancing on that first day, we would have gained most of the territory we now hold, and saved thousands of lives. You do realise this is the third time we have tried to achieve these same goals, and each time we ended up with the same tragic results.'

'Yes, but this time it is different. This time we have more men, more cannons, more tanks and airplanes. Surely, we must prevail.'

They went quiet after that. Once again, both men remained entrenched in their own opinions.

On September 20th, the Australians joined in the third battle of Ypres. They started their attack through the splintered remains of Polygon Wood.

'The Germans have pill-boxes protecting their

machine guns, Lieutenant. How are we supposed to take them out?' Sergeant Jones asked.

'We just have to get close enough to use our bomb throwers, or we have to call in the artillery,' Lieutenant Williams replied.

'Our communication lines to the rear have been cut by their artillery.'

'We just have to do the best we can, Sergeant.'

From the day that the Australians had arrived, the shelling from both sides had not stopped. It had taken a heavy toll on both sides, and Lieutenant Williams' shaking had started again, and he could not control it. His head had now started to shake as well as his hands.

'Are you all right, Sir? Do you want to go to the rear?'

'No. I'll be over this soon enough, Sergeant. Can you tell the men that we must keep advancing? When they take fire from a machine gun nest, they are to take cover in the shell holes, but they must keep advancing from shell hole to shell hole. Tell them to try and get close enough to use the new bombs they have been trained to use. We must take out those machine guns, Sergeant.'

'Yes, Sir.'

Because one side of the Australian advance was slowed, it split the line and exposed the men to enfilade fire from German machine guns, which tore into them with devastating effect. As well as this, the German artillery continued to pound the advancing Australians. After just over a week of heavy fighting, the Australians had suffered almost 11 000 casualties.

Lieutenant Williams sat in a shell crater with Sergeant Jones. Williams was shaking badly but refused to leave his platoon. Jones admired him for this but still thought he should retire. Jones kept his opinion to himself, however, not knowing what he would do if he were in his lieutenant's place.

'My God, Sergeant, when will this stop?'

Sergeant Jones shook his head but did not reply.

'Well, there's nothing else for it. We'll just have to keep going.'

Having said that, Lieutenant Williams rose out of the crater and began advancing once again. Sergeant Jones and the rest of the platoon followed.

Artillery shells screamed overhead and exploded with large eruptions of earth, which blew Australian soldiers in all directions. Suddenly, an artillery shell exploded in their midst. One man disappeared, torn apart by the explosion, and two others began writhing in agony. One had his belly split open and was trying to hold his bowels and put them back into his abdomen. The other had deep cuts to his arms and legs, which spurted blood, while he tried to hold his flesh together.

As Lieutenant Williams stood looking at this carnage, his head, arms and legs began jerking uncontrollably.

'Sir, we have to take shelter!' Sergeant Jones shouted to him. 'Over here, Sir. There's a crater.'

The whole platoon had taken cover once the artillery had found its range. Finally, Sergeant Jones pulled Lieutenant Williams—who continued to jerk violently—into the crater. It was clear to Sergeant Jones that Lieutenant Williams was unable to continue, so he called for stretcher bearers and had him taken from the field of battle.

On October 4th, the Australians captured Broodseinde Ridge, but then it began to rain again. On October 12th, they started their final assault on the village of Passchendaele, atop the main ridge, but the Germans were not going to give up this vital strategic land cheaply.

Under wretched conditions and with appalling casualties, the Australians eventually became exhausted, and could do no more. They had taken ground and lost it several times.

'We can't go any further, Sergeant. We don't have enough men left, and those we do have are exhausted after all this fighting. Besides, the Germans keep counterattacking. Our advance has stalled,' the platoon corporal said.

'Yes, surely our commanders know that. Why do they keep us here? We need to be relieved,' Sergeant Jones replied.

'They must think we can do more, but they are not with us, and they have not been with us from the start of this bloody impossible attack.'

They both went silent after that. It was the first time that Sergeant Jones had ever heard his men openly admit that they had had enough.

Word eventually came through that the Canadians were going to relieve them, and on November 15th, the Australians left Passchendaele for the relative safety of the reserve line.

Not long after the Canadian relief, and the taking of Passchendaele, the third battle of Ypres came to an end. It had cost the Allies approximately 300 000 casualties (thirty-five men for every metre gained) and the Germans a further 260 000 casualties.

'Well, Charles, should we go out and celebrate our 'great' victory?' asked one of the officers at Headquarters.

'Surely, even you can see that we had to try. This push could have won the war for us, and the weather was against us. Don't forget that. Who could have predicted such bad weather?'

'Oh, I see. So now God is conspiring against us?'

'Don't be a fool, man. I know we have little to show for our effort. I know we did not achieve our objectives, but surely that is irrelevant. We started the battle with everything in our favour. We had the technology. We had the manpower. It was just unfortunate that we ran into some unfavourable conditions.'

'Unfortunate? Unfavourable conditions? Good God, man, can you hear yourself? You do realise we have lost over 300,000 men trying to achieve what we had failed to achieve twice before. You do realise that, don't you?'

'Yes, and that is truly unfortunate, but I still think it was worth a go. We had so much going for us.'

Charles' counterpart stood speechless; his mouth remained open and he raised his eyebrows. He was about to say something but changed his mind. Instead, he quietly walked away, shaking his head in disbelief.

After Ann had finally got a break from the hospital and returned home for a good night's sleep, she felt refreshed and went down for her breakfast the next morning. Joan was waiting for her and gave her Charles' letter. Ann opened and read the letter quietly to herself. Joan also sat quietly, waiting for Ann to say something about her son's news. When Ann folded the letter and put it to her side, Joan became annoyed.

'What does Charles say, my Dear?'

'Charles told me that he wants to separate from me,' Ann replied matter-of-factly.

'What? May I see the letter, please?'

Ann passed the letter to Joan whose face twitched in anger as she read it. Then she looked up at the ceiling and sniffed loudly. Finally, she looked down at Ann.

'This is incredible,' she began. 'I didn't know you and

Charles were having a problem with your marriage. I simply can't believe he would do something like this. No one in this family has ever been separated before. Well, there was his cousin, but she was a wayward and wilful child. Charles, on the other hand, had a quality upbringing. Our class of people just don't get separated.'

Ann was left astonished. Here she was in this vulnerable position with Charles, and all Joan was concerned about were appearance and class. What Ann needed right now was reassurance that her future would be viable without Charles, because she knew that Charles was not the type to change his mind. Now that he had decided to do this, he would go through with it.

'Do you want me to move out now?' Ann asked.

'No, Dear. I will contact Charles and sort this out. Something must have happened to bring about his change of mind, and I will find out what it is and fix it. Don't worry, Dear, your marriage will be safe.'

Do I really want it to be safe? Ann thought to herself. Was Charles right? Had they drifted too far apart in the last several years? And there was the lengthy separation brought about by the war. Would it be best to just end it and make a fresh start away from each other? Ann could not answer these questions right now, she needed time to think them through.

'Thank you. I must leave for work now, but could we talk about it some more when I get home tonight?'

'Yes, Dear, of course. Will you be able to perform your duties today?'

Ann thought about that for a while but realised she wanted to be at work, away from here, where she could think this through on her own.

'Yes. Don't worry, I'll be all right.'

'You are a strong girl, Ann. I have always admired you for that.'

Again, Ann was caught by surprise. That was the first time Joan had ever praised her. It felt strange and left her a little unsettled. Having to think of Joan as a confidant was something Ann could not handle right now.

'Thank you for that, Mother,' Ann replied.

As Ann rose from the breakfast table to leave for work, she noticed a smile cross Joan's lips. Then she realised that was the first time she had called Joan 'Mother'. She wondered if she had made a mistake but realised it was a reasonable reaction, given the circumstances of the morning.

At the hospital, her mind was unsettled all day. She

continued to wonder about her future with Charles. She began to think that Charles was right. It would be better to start new lives for themselves. She also knew that separation was not such a rare thing in England. Perhaps not as much in their social circle, but it happened all the time in the lower classes, she believed, and who was to say they were not right and the middle classes wrong? Still, she also knew that some in their circle would believe that both Charles' and her characters lacked moral certitude, but she began to contemplate starting her life anew and found that appealing—now that Charles had made it a possibility. The chance for a new and better life was something that she now saw herself moving towards.

During the course of the day, as she was treating her patients, her mind went to Peter. She was sure there was a strong attraction between the two of them, but Peter had been transferred out to a rehabilitation centre without the two of them even agreeing to keep in touch. Now he was probably on his way back to France, so there was little chance of her seeing him again. She wished she had not discouraged him so much when she felt he was trying to take their relationship beyond the nurse-patient arrangement. Back then it would have been improper, but now she felt she could have agreed to keep in touch with him at least. Knowing that a man still saw her as a 'good prospect' boosted her self-esteem, and she would take as much of that as she could right now. That night, when she had returned home from the hospital, Joan was waiting to greet her.

'I have written to Charles and explained to him that separation is not possible. I also asked him what was really behind his request,' she explained.

'What do you mean? Didn't he say that we had drifted apart?'

'Oh that, Dear. You don't really think that is the real reason, do you?'

'Well, what do you think is the real reason?'

'In matters like this—oh, and I do mean this with no disrespect to you, my Dear—but experience has taught me that it is usually another woman.'

'Oh, I see. But Charles is busy with the war and all. Surely that can't be it?'

'Soldiers go on leave, Dear, and those French women can seduce even the strongest-willed men.'

'Well, you were very fast in writing. I'm now beginning to agree with Charles, that it would be better for both of us if we were to separate,' Ann replied.

'You can't mean that, Ann. Separation leaves such a social stigma, especially for someone like you.'

'What do you mean, *someone like me?*'

'Well, Dear … how can I put this delicately? You are not a young woman anymore, and Charles was a climb up for you. I hate to mention it like this, but how do you expect to support yourself?'

Ann's body stiffened.

'I have my job at the hospital, and after the war I expect there will be a need for someone with my skills,' she replied, annoyance highlighting her tone.

'Yes, I see. You are a working woman, but do you really want to continue working for the rest of your life?' Joan went on, oblivious to Ann's feelings.

'Of course. Even if Charles and I were to remain together, I would still want to continue working in a hospital somewhere, if they will let me. It is very rewarding and satisfying.'

'Yes, Dear, but things change. You may not feel that way in a few years' time.'

'Forgive me, but didn't you imply that Charles may have been unfaithful to me? What do you expect me to do if that is true?'

'Believe me, Dear, these affairs of the heart die out in

time. They cannot be sustained. Besides, Charles will return home to England and she will still be in France. No, if he is having an affair, it cannot last, and you would be foolish to throw away your marriage for the sake of a wartime fling.'

'So, you are saying that I should ignore this and carry on as if nothing has happened?'

'Exactly so, my Dear. Exactly so.'

'Maybe that is good advice, but maybe it is good for Charles and me to try for a new life without each other.'

'I see. So, you really are open to a separation?'

'Well, what I am saying is to leave that open for now—until we find out what is actually going on with Charles.'

'Well, that's sensible. So, we wait until Charles replies to my letter. Would that be agreeable with you?'

'Yes, I would be happy to see how Charles replies to your letter.'

With that said, Ann went up to her room to freshen up for dinner.

* * *

Casualties from the 'big push' arrived at the First Australian Auxiliary Hospital as a trickle, which later developed into a flood. Ann was there to greet them all.

A tent had been set up on the lawn outside the hospital to act as a reception and triage centre because the hospital had become overcrowded, with stretchers even filling the hallways. Some patients had been sent over from the 3rd Australian General Hospital in France as fully-treated patients, while others were in a raw state and needed urgent attention.

As Ann worked through the casualties, she noticed a young lieutenant standing at the back of the tent, his head lowered and his body shaking and twitching uncontrollably. Ann had seen cases like this before. They called it 'shell shock'. She knew his mind could not take the shock of war any longer, so his body had started twitching and jerking in an attempt to end his suffering. She also knew he would be feeling guilty about being here among the badly wounded veterans, but she could not get to see him until she had worked her way through the more urgent cases.

Ann worked steadily through her patients until most of them had been treated or placed in the hospital; then she went to see her CO and told him of the young lieutenant suffering from shell shock. They both agreed that he should be transferred to a hospital that specialised in treating his condition. Ann made inquiries and was able to place him in such a facility. After that, she went to see Lieutenant Williams.

'How are you feeling, Lieutenant?' she asked him.

'Oh, I'm fine really. Just this damn twitching.'

'Yes. You're suffering from what we call shell shock, and there are places that specialise in treating your condition. Unfortunately, there is very little we can do for you here.'

'Oh, I see.'

'Yes. I have made inquiries and we would like to transfer you to one of those places.'

'I see.'

'Yes, Lieutenant. With your permission, I will go and make arrangements for your transfer.'

'Yes. Thank you, Sister.'

Ann went and contacted the Seale Hayne Hospital in Devon and arranged Lieutenant Williams' transfer.

When he arrived at Seale Hayne, which was a three-story red-brick building with many windows and a large stone entrance, Craig was put under the care of Dr Allan Hall, who had adopted an enlightened way of treating shell shock victims.

During the early years of the war, shell shock was

seen as an emotional weakness and even as cowardice. Some victims were charged with desertion, cowardice or insubordination; others were not only charged but subjected to a mock trial and executed. Australian soldiers, on the other hand, were never executed, not even for desertion. Billy Hughes, the Prime Minister of Australia, saw such treatment of soldiers as barbaric, and had banned it, much to the consternation of the British High Command, who believed it would erode the fighting capacity of the soldiers. The Australians proved that the British belief was groundless.

Dr Hall did not accept that his patients lacked anything in their characters and treated them with humanity and dignity. He believed in taking his patients to the countryside to work on farms, the use of hypnosis to get to the root of his patients' problems and encouraging them to write and produce a magazine with a gossip column called 'Ward Whispers'.

Within a short time, this approach led to the relaxation of his patients, who eventually became cured of their twitching, depression and general state of confusion and withdrawal.

After just two weeks of treatment, Lieutenant Craig Williams was sitting one day in Dr Hall's office.

'How are you feeling today, Craig?'

'Much better, thank you.'

'How is the twitching going?'

'Much better now.'

'You know, you can probably cure it altogether.'

'Really?'

'Yes. Once you recognise the source of your problem, you should be able to control it.'

'What is the source?'

'Do you remember that soldier in your platoon, who got a stomach wound and spilled his intestines?'

'Yes. I have nightmares about that incident.'

'Yes. A lot of our victims are lieutenants who lead their platoons into battle. Subconsciously they believe that because they led the soldiers under their command into battle, they are responsible for the injuries suffered by those soldiers. You fall into that category, Craig. You led them, so you blame yourself for all that happens to them. That is why your hand started shaking and when you saw that young soldier with his intestines spilled out, you cracked. Your mind could no longer take the guilt and blame. That was the point beyond which you could not go on leading young men to their fate, because you believed it was not fate but rather your fault that these things kept happening. Our hypnosis sessions have highlighted this, and this is the incident you must now face and conquer.'

'I see … and how do I do that?'

'By consciously telling yourself that it is not your fault, whenever you have guilty feelings. You can tell yourself that you were only following orders, or you can blame the war itself. The simple fact is that young men die or get wounded in war, and this has nothing to do with your leadership.'

'I have thought that before, but it did not help.'

'That's because you do not believe that it has nothing to do with you. Your subconscious wants you to go on punishing yourself. You must go beyond telling yourself, to believing what you tell yourself.'

'How do I do that?'

'There's no magic formula for that, I'm afraid.'

'Oh. So, you can't help me to believe my conscious thoughts?'

'It all depends on what works for you. You could take a leaf out of religious belief though.'

'How do you mean?'

'Well, some religions have survived for centuries because their memberships believe in their church's teachings. Now you must teach yourself to believe.'

'How do I do that?'

'By telling yourself over and over again that it is not your fault whenever those visions come back to you.'

'I see. And this will lead to my believing it?'

'Yes, it will. It also might help if you develop some little habit to perform whenever you tell yourself that it is not your fault.'

'Like what?'

'Well, the Catholics pass a rosary through their fingers, but maybe you could just rub your forefinger and thumb together—like this.' Dr Hall demonstrated the action to Craig. 'Why don't you try it now with me?'

They both completed the action together while repeating the words: 'It's not my fault. It's not my fault. I am a victim like everyone else. It's not my fault.'

'If you say that enough times, you will convince yourself of its truth.' Dr Hall said persuasively.

With the session ended, Craig went back to his room and practiced his new habit over and over. He wanted desperately to be healed, and if this would do it for him, then he would practice it religiously.

Two more weeks of working on the farm—digging and turning soil for garden beds, working with farm animals and carrying out general repairs to the various sheds and machinery that were a part of the farm—helped Craig relax and get past his tormented spirit. Whenever he felt himself slipping into old habits, he repeated the mantra demonstrated by Dr Hall.

After just two weeks, he was astonished at how cured he had become. He could stand and walk naturally, and whenever his hand started shaking he simply repeated his new routine until the shaking faded. He was so grateful to Dr Hall for his recovery that he went to see the doctor and thanked him personally.

'You are welcome, Craig. Do you think you are ready to resume your duties?'

'Gosh, I don't know about that. What do you think?'

'That's not up to me, Craig. That's something you have to decide for yourself.'

'Yes, that makes sense. Well, I guess I'm as ready as I ever will be.'

'I think it best if we get you posted to some duties behind the front line.'

'I don't want to shirk on my mates.'

'There you go, blaming yourself again. You know you have to stop beating yourself up. I want to arrange this for you, but you will have to agree to it.'

'Yes, all right then. I suppose that is better than not going back at all.'

'That's the spirit. I'm sure you are making the right decision.'

After his recovery, Lieutenant Peter Bowen had spent two weeks on recreational leave in London before being promoted to captain and posted to General John Monash's HQ in France. He still had a slight limp in his right leg and had developed the habit of using a walking stick, which enabled him to walk faster. His injury had ensured he would not be given an active role in one of the battalions. But the chronic shortage of manpower in the Australian ranks, owing to the drop of recruitment back home and the heavy losses on the front, had meant not only that Australian battalions were left seriously undermanned but also that Peter would not be sent home.

By the time Peter joined General Monash's HQ staff, preparations for the Battle of Hamel were well underway. The British High Command had put General Monash in full command of the planning and execution of the attack, and his staff had been busy over the last couple of weeks putting it all together.

In preparation for the coming attack, airplanes flew over German trenches daily, dropping bombs, while tanks drew up closer to the front lines under cover from the noise of the airplane's engines. Artillery batteries also fired smoke and gas on the enemy trenches, forcing the Germans to put on their gas masks. When the real assault came, only smoke would be landed on the Germans. It was hoped that the Germans, expecting gas, would put on their gas masks, thus making them less effective in resisting the Australian assault, while the smoke would give the Australians cover for their attack. Also, some American troops had been posted with the Australians to make up for the shortage in Australian manpower.

Peter's job was to co-ordinate all the reports coming into Monash's HQ and to present General Monash with an overall summary of the situation. One day, Peter overheard General Monash reporting to his superiors. In his report, General Monash likened his battle plan to a delicately-balanced symphony, with all the sections of the orchestra playing their part in time and completing their assigned segments as expected, to produce the overall performance.

'The German spring offensive created a bulge in the line here at Hamel,' Major Smith, who was Peter's immediate superior, said. 'Consequently, the Germans can observe our troop movements and cover our trenches with enfilading fire. Our objective is to retake Hamel and straighten out this bulge.'

'I see,' Peter replied. 'So, this is not another big push?'

'No. This is the small bite approach, which has been circulating throughout High Command for some time now. All the battalions' objectives are clearly set out. Your job is to check that they are fully aware of their objectives and keep a running report as to how those objectives are being met.'

'Yes, Sir.'

'Do you have any questions?'

'Well, I need to know what the objectives are.'

'You will be fully briefed by Captain Johnston.'

With that said, Major Smith left Peter and Captain Johnston took over. After the briefing, Peter was fully aware of every aspect of the operation and was eager to get down to the battalions and go through it with the battalion COs.

One big change to Monash's approach was that he wanted his troops to advance under the protection of cannons, machine guns, tanks, mortars and airplanes. The new Mark V tanks, which were an improvement over the earlier disappointing versions, it was hoped, would make a considerable difference to the upcoming battle. The battle would be a dawn attack, bringing to bear combined arms for a concerted effort. Monash's planning had been meticulous, and he calculated that the objectives of all divisions would be met within just ninety minutes.

On the day of the battle, all the pieces of the operation came together as they were expected to. At 10:30 pm on July 3rd, sixty British tanks started their final journey to the front line, under the covering noise of British planes, which droned overhead of the German lines, dropping bombs. The planes flew three missions each and continued their activity until the artillery opened fire at 3:00 am. Over 600 British and French guns pounded the German lines, dropping live shells and smoke canisters.

Back at HQ, Peter was getting reports that all was going as planned. The feint attack at Ville-sur-Ancre had been used to draw German support away from Hamel.

At 3:10 am the troops rose out of their trenches and set off under the cover of a rolling artillery barrage. The troops moved just sixty-nine metres short of the barrage. Some shells fell short, killing some of the attacking troops. These were the first casualties that Peter heard about, and he was saddened by the news. He had seen troops killed by 'friendly fire' before. *Such a waste,* he thought.

The clouds of smoke and dust that had now become the battlefield made it difficult for the battalions to see their objectives, and some of the tanks got separated from the battalions they were supposed to support. In these instances, when the attacking troops began to encounter heavy machine gun fire from the German lines, Lewis gun teams sprang into action. There were two Lewis gun teams to each platoon and they went into a prone position and returned fire on the German machine gun nests. This gave the attacking troops cover for their assault.

When the tanks were in support of the attacking troops, they were used on the German machine gun nests. The tanks engaged the German nests with six-pound cannons or their own machine guns. Sometimes they simply ran over the top of the machine gun nests with their tracks. The tanks were also used to flatten barbed wire entanglements.

Sixty British Mark V tanks and four supply tanks were used in the attack on Hamel. They were a marked improvement over the earlier versions, which were subject to mechanical failure, and were less manoeuvrable than the Mark V. One improvement was that the soldier giving directions to the tank driver walked behind the tank rather than in front as was the previous practice. He was connected to the driver by a cable with a handset at one end, into which he shouted his directions. On the other end was the driver who wore a headset so he could hear the directions over the noise of the tank's roaring engine. The tanks also had coloured diagrams painted on their sides, which corresponded with the battalions they were supporting. Consequently, the battalions knew which tanks to follow—something that had been a problem in the past, when the tanks had become separated from the troops they were supporting.

Various means were used to keep the reports coming in to Peter. These means included rockets (although not very successful), pigeons, runners and even the new wireless technology. All reports were the same: positive. The battle of Hamel was proceeding as planned. Finally, reports came back that objectives were being met; the battle came to an end after just ninety-three minutes. The Germans had been successfully driven back from Hamel, and the Australian troops began mopping-up operations and rebuilding the shattered defences. Several tanks were used to resupply the troops with ammunition, fresh water and hot food. Planes were also used to parachute in supplies. The troops were delighted by this turn of events, as they were used to getting resupplied late.

The Battle of Hamel was a small but significant victory. It showed conclusively the effectiveness of using combined arms tactics against entrenched opposition. As such, it was studied carefully and adapted throughout the remainder of the war, bringing to an end the domination of the machine gun against frontal attacks.

The next day, when Peter and his aide walked the battlefield, Peter was surprised at how few casualties there had been. Most of the wounded had been removed from the field. The dead still littered the ground, but there were fewer of them than Peter had experienced in the past.

Suddenly, the Germans opened up with their artillery. Shells began bursting all around them.

'Here we go again!' Peter yelled, diving for a shell creator. His aide followed quickly behind him, while hundreds of shells continued to explode on the trenches nearby.

Peter had known that a German counterattack would happen at any moment. He also knew that the Germans would likely use a gas attack. He hoped that his own troops were dug in sufficiently to stop the attack.

Peter and his aide put on their gas masks just before the familiar clanging sound warned them of a gas attack. Peter had seen men who had suffered from gas. They often went into convulsions and went black in the face and throat. A blood-soaked, foamy sort of jelly erupted from their mouths as they groaned into a lingering death. Such a fate, Peter promised himself, would not happen to him. He had vowed to end his own life if he ever got gassed.

For now, they would have to get out of the crater they were in because gas always flowed into the lowest spots on the field, and that meant shell craters would quickly fill up with gas.

They ran back towards their headquarters, seeking shelter as they went. When the shelling stopped, the German counterattack erupted behind them. They dived into an empty machine gun pit for protection. The pit had been taken out by one of their tanks. Most of the German defenders had been machine-gunned, but one of them had been flattened. It was a sorry sight to see a dead soldier in that condition; even his helmet had been squashed flat. Peter withdrew his gaze and concentrated on the battle in front of them.

With his field glasses he could see the determined resistance of the Australian troops, supported by British tanks, and Australian mortars and machine guns. Allied artillery also opened fire on the attackers, who at first halted and then withdrew from the field.

Peter knew that he had to get back to HQ before the reports started to come in about the successful repulsion of the counterattack. Overall, the Battle of Hamel had been a resounding success and Peter's final report would have to reflect that.

After the battle, when things had settled down and Peter had some spare time on his hands, he wrote to Ann thanking her for saving his leg. He also told her that he appreciated all that she had done for him. He told her of his new posting and that he enjoyed the work he was doing, now that the high casualty rates were down.

He left her with his postal address and hoped that she would correspond with him. He didn't know how she would react to his letter, but he was hopeful that she would reply.

* * *

'I'm glad we can have this time together to speak freely about your problem with Charles,' Joan Copley said.

Ann had come home early so she and Joan could have this conversation. Joan had told her that she had news about Charles.

'My problem? I thought Charles wanted a separation. That's hardly my problem.'

'Yes, Dear, of course. Nevertheless, it is a problem for both of you. Don't you agree?'

Ann took a deep breath. Was this going to become an exchange of recriminations? She decided to get right to the point.

'You said you have news from Charles.'

'Yes, it is as I suspected. There is another woman. He has this fantasy about living with her in Paris after the war.'

Ann felt the pain of betrayal sweep through her body. She clenched her fists and locked her jaw.

'I see. Well, I guess that is not just grounds for a separation. Perhaps a divorce would be more in order.'

'But surely you don't want that, Ann? If you are just patient, all this will blow over and Charles will come home to us. These affairs never last. You need to be patient, my Dear.'

'Why? What if I agree with Charles? What if I really want to go ahead with a divorce or a separation?'

'Don't be hasty, Ann. Too much is riding on this. You have your whole life in front of you.'

Ann shifted her weight from foot to foot. She was fed up with all this nonsense about her becoming the suffering martyr, while Charles continued to ignore their marriage. Surely, she was entitled to some consideration. After all, it was not as though she could not forge a life of her own. She had her work and she was still attractive. She would not have to be alone for long, if she wanted it that way. It would probably do Charles a service to leave him. Maybe then his conscience could be clear, although he had not shown much of a conscience to date.

Ann had had time to think a lot about her marriage to Charles, and now that he had another woman, she felt free to indulge herself a little.

'I don't want to wait around for Charles to come to his

senses, Joan. He has made his own decision, and now I'll make mine. I want a separation at least.'

'You can't mean that, Ann. All over a silly infidelity. Don't you know this happens all the time? Most men cheat on their wives, but that doesn't lead to a separation. Please don't do anything rash at this time. Please wait a little longer. This is a wartime fling after all. Let's wait until the end of the war, when you will see Charles again. Can you do that for me please?'

'No. I agree that I need to see Charles, but I won't wait until the end of the war. I'll put in for a tour of duty in France and see Charles when I am there. That's when we can both make up our minds.' Ann said it with such finality that Joan merely nodded her head in agreement.

Two weeks later, Ann was posted to a casualty clearing station (CCS) behind the Australian line. She had been sent there to instruct the CCS nurses in the Carrel-Dakin treatment of wounds. Two weeks after that, she was given a four-day leave pass and had taken a train to Paris. Now she stood on the platform of the Gare du Nord railway station, awaiting the arrival of Charles' train.

She had her hair pulled straight back from her forehead and she had applied little makeup, preferring instead to rely on her naturally white complexion. During the cold, her cheeks took on a ruddy appearance, which meant she seldom applied any rouge. Her features were set, with no hint of excited expectancy, which most of the other females on the platform exhibited. She was nervous and kept fidgeting with her overnight bag, slung over her shoulder.

She wondered what Charles would say and kept thinking about their life together—how much in love they were at first but how they had drifted apart, and after the death of their child, how they no longer seemed to care for each other.

Charles finally arrived and their reunion was a cold one. Charles merely walked up to her and told her that he was happy to have this time together to sort out their separation. Then he suggested they move to a café where they could continue their conversation in private.

Ann noticed how their reunion differed so much from almost all other couples on the platform. Charles and Ann had merely stood opposite each other without touching while Charles did all the talking, whereas most other couples had embraced and smiled and chattered. She felt sad that Charles and she had lost so much but resolved within herself that she would see this through.

Charles took Ann to a café off the main road where they were alone.

'So, you are happy for us to have a separation?' Charles asked.

So much like Charles, Ann thought. Straight to the point. She could see that they would have little to say about their life together. All Charles seemed interested in was to get this over with. Well, she would accommodate him.

'Yes, I think it best for both of us. I feel sorry for your mother though. She will be alone now if you move to Paris.'

'Yes, well it will be difficult for her at first, but I'm sure she will get used to it in time.'

Charles said it so matter-of-factly that Ann was taken aback. She closed her eyes and shook her head. *How cold Charles has become,* she thought. *How callous.* She wanted to slap him across the face, but she calmed herself. She would not let him rile her. After all, she now wanted this separation as much as he did.

'I suppose you're right,' she said, just as coldly. 'Do you

intend to visit your mother now and then?' She tried not to sound sarcastic.

'Yes, I suppose so. I'm sure that my business will take me to London from time to time.'

There it was again. His callousness. Couldn't he just visit with his mother for her sake alone? Why did he have to mix it with business? Ann wondered how many other men were like Charles. Quite a few, she imagined. She began to wonder what she had seen in Charles in the first place, but then she remembered how attentive he had been to her needs at first. Now, it was all about his needs.

Their coffee arrived and they sat quietly sipping at it, neither knowing what more there was to say.

'I must say, Charles, that I was shocked by this news at first. I couldn't understand why you would want a separation, but now that I know there is another woman involved, I can see the need for it.'

Ann was determined to show Charles that she could be just as cold as he. Charles did not reply. He merely sat quietly, looking out at the road. Finally, he turned back to Ann.

'Yes, well, the less said about that the better,' he said.

I can't believe the nerve of this man, Ann thought.

She felt disgust at Charles and decided to end their conversation before she lost her temper.

'I'm going now, Charles,' she said, getting to her feet. 'You have what you wanted. I hope we can both find happiness in the future.'

'Yes. I do wish you well, Ann.'

Ann stood looking down on Charles, who stood up. She smiled and said goodbye. She did not offer either her hand or her cheek, rather she merely put her overnight bag on her shoulder, turned and walked away. She would find a nice little hotel around here and spend some time alone. After that, she would take in the sights of Paris.

Chrles walked away, in a hurry to meet up with Yvette. *That went well,* he thought. *Now to tell Yvette the good news.*

In August, the Allies unleashed a one-hundred-day armoured offensive against the German lines, which became known as the Battle of Amiens. Using armour and artillery in support of attacking infantry, the battle was a resounding success for the Allies and put an end to the trench warfare, which had been fought on the western front for the previous four years. The Allied offensive was so successful that German General Ludendorff described the first day of the battle as, 'the black day of the German army'. Convinced that Germany could not win the war, Generals Ludendorff and Hindenburg allowed the Reichstag (Germany's parliament) to take control of the German Government and enter into peace talks with the Allies to end WWI.

All this was great news for General Monash's HQ, where Peter picked up on the enthusiasm that pervaded the HQ. Peter's reports showed not only the success of the attacking units but also the record number of surrendering German soldiers.

Peter could feel this terrible conflict coming to a close. When he carried out his battlefield inspection, he noticed the similarity between this battlefield and that of Hamel. Machine gun pits had been overrun or strafed by advancing Allied tanks and craters marked the creeping barrage laid down by Allied artillery. As he pushed forward to catch up with the still-advancing front line, he could smell the battlefield. Cordite and smoke filled the air. Eventually, he came in contact with a Major Sawyers, who noticed Peter's red tape around his cap, signalling that Peter was part of Monash's HQ.

'Good morning, Sir,' Peter greeted his superior with a smile.

'Good morning, Captain.'

'This seems to be going well,' Peter continued.

'Yes, only two problems—we are advancing beyond the support of our artillery, and we are having to deal with thousands of surrendering Germans.'

'Yes, has that slowed your progress?'

'Definitely. We need to get the artillery up quicker than we have been doing and we need extra troops to escort the surrendering Germans to the rear. Otherwise, we'll just have to point them in the direction of our rear and hope that they follow through.'

'Umm … well, I'll mention that in my next report when I get back to HQ.'

'Good.'

'Did the resupply of ammunition and hot food get through?'

'Yes, that was well organised and helped us a lot.'

'Thank you for your time, Sir. I won't keep you.'

The Major disappeared into the fog of the battlefield. Peter knew that the Germans would eventually regroup and counterattack, but there was no evidence of that happening in the near future, so he returned to his HQ, where he compiled his report and handed it to his superior. After that, he sat thinking about what he had witnessed. It was clear now that the war would not last much longer, and he began to wonder what he would do when it all came to an end.

* * *

Craig had been posted to the military attaché for the Australian Embassy in Paris. This posting had been made possible because the serving lieutenant there had requested a transfer to the front. The crisis in manpower at the front had ensured his transfer and Craig's service made him an acceptable replacement.

The Australian Embassy was located on the rue Jean Roy, which led onto the Quai Branly, running parallel with the river Seine. From his office, Craig could see the Eiffel Tower, where he often took his lunch. Surrounding the tower was a large park. It was well kept, with a large paved area and grassy surrounds. Trees provided shade and flowering shrubs a peaceful ambiance. The ordered and neatly manicured park provided Craig with a balance to his troubled mind, so he was always happy when he lunched there.

He had also taken up the habit of attending church services on Sunday evenings, when he was not required for duty. He went to a nearby church where he took communion with a small number of parishioners. Once again, the ordered nature of the ceremony provided his mind with a calmness, which led him to a welcome peace of mind.

All in all, he had made a successful transformation from the broken soldier he had been only a few months earlier. He still got the shakes now and then but was able to control it with his mantra. Whenever the shakes attacked him, he would find a quiet spot and recant his lines. Gradually, a calmness would descend upon him, and slowly he worked his way back to normal. He was happy with where he was at and looked forward to a next-to-normal future.

Captain Scott, Craig's immediate superior at the Embassy, was a man who drank a lot. This left Craig with the added responsibility of seeing to the everyday running of the military attaché. Guard duty was the most important aspect of his work, so he spent many hours making sure that the soldiers under his command were fit and well turned out. Their uniforms had to be clean and neatly pressed, their webbing and equipment polished, and their boots shining. Their fitness regimen required Craig to participate in many hours of exercise and running, both around the courtyard inside the Embassy and the Parisian streets outside. Finally, he had to ensure that his soldiers were sticking to their duty roster. This meant inspections and getting to know not only their names, but something of their attitudes and personalities. Craig's efforts were rewarded with a well-run and functioning military attaché, where soldiers were kept busy and out of trouble.

The attaché's warrant officer was the person who

filled out all the reports and kept the unit's paperwork in order. Captain Scott would appear at the office late in the morning, sign any material put before him by his warrant officer, take a couple of drinks from his private stash, then retire to a nearby hotel lounge, where he would drink until it closed.

Craig sometimes wondered about Captain Scott's drinking problem—whether he drank to soothe his nerves or was just an alcoholic who couldn't get off the wagon. Whatever his reasons for drinking, however, the warrant officer and Craig picked up the slack created by their CO. At one time, Craig questioned Captain Scott about his drinking and was told to mind his own business. Captain Scott became indignant and defensive, and Craig was forced to back away from furthering his inquiry. Craig was sure that the unit could function perfectly well without its CO and knew that their superiors would eventually catch up with Captain Scott—they always did—so he decided to let it go for now. Besides, to make a formal complaint would only put him in a bad light. In the meantime, he would continue to do his best to keep the unit fully functional. Nevertheless, he did wish that Captain Scott would take a greater interest in the running of his unit. Craig was certain the men would appreciate hearing from their CO now and then, just to keep a better organisational merit for the unit and better communication between the men and those appointed to lead them. It was certain that if not for Craig and his insistence on 'spit and polish', the unit would quickly turn into a poorly-run attaché, with the men falling into lazy habits.

It was clear that the men picked up on those who led them, and when a leader failed in his duty, it usually began a rot, which set in, eventually running throughout the unit. Craig's hard work in keeping the men busy and focused on their duties, however, was the short circuit to any failing that might creep into the military attaché to the Australian Embassy in Paris.

In his time off, Craig liked to get away from the Embassy. He tended to gravitate to those places where he could be alone with his thoughts. He sometimes walked to the Champs-Élysées where he took coffee at one of the sidewalk cafés. The coffee was black and hot, and he took it with a square of dark chocolate, as was the French custom.

Craig was surprised at how alone he could feel in the midst of so many people passing him by. The sidewalk café placed him near so many people, yet he was able to think private thoughts about himself and his current life. He enjoyed his work at the Embassy. It gave him a sense of accomplishment when his soldiers were able to fulfil their duties. He also began to wonder what his life would be like after the war. Would he be able to continue controlling his shell shock, or would it return to incapacitate him? Would he be able to stay on at the Embassy, or would he return home to an uncertain future?

At his local church, Craig noticed a young woman in the congregation. She always sat towards the back, where he also sat. He often wondered what her life was like. She never attended with anyone else, again like Craig, and was respectful throughout the service. She seemed earnest in her devotion and this piqued Craig's curiosity, which grew and grew, until one day when he saw her on a park bench near the Eiffel Tower, he decided to approach her.

'Bonjour, Mademoiselle. Parles-tu anglaise?'

'Hello. Yes, I speak English. Can I help you?'

'Well, my name is Craig and I work at the Australian Embassy here in Paris. I hope you don't mind me approaching you like this, but I have noticed you at church.'

'Yes. Is there something I can do for you?'

'Well, I just wanted to take my lunch with you. Would that be all right?'

She accepted his offer. Craig continued to talk to her.

'It is really beautiful here. I come as often as I can. Do you come here often?' he asked.

'Why yes, I do. I like it here. You see, my father used to bring me to the church nearby, where you saw me, and then after the service we would take our lunch here in the park near the Eiffel Tower. It was a happy part of my childhood and that's what keeps bringing me back.'

'Are you close with your father?'

'Yes, I was. But he passed away three years ago. I have no family now. My mother left us when I was a child and I haven't seen her since. I don't know what became of her.'

'Was your father in the war?'

'Yes, that's how he died. He volunteered when the Germans invaded France. He was a transport driver, and his truck was blown up delivering ammunition to the front.' She said it with a tone of finality in her voice that startled Craig. *Such a fatalistic view of life,* he thought.

'I'm sorry to hear that,' he said.

'Oh, it seems so long ago now. So much has happened to me since then that I seldom think about it anymore. I try to keep only the happy memories now.'

They went into a silence, while Craig tried to process all that this pretty, young woman had said to him. *So much suffering in her life. How does she keep it all together?* he wondered.

Her face lit up at Craig's attention. She crossed her legs, and a smile came over her face.

'May I ask what your name is?' Craig eventually asked.

'Yvette Blanc.' She paused for a moment, then went on. 'Do you like it here?' she asked.

'Oh, yes,' Craig replied. 'I often take my lunch here—it's so full of life. So many people seem happy and enjoying themselves—so different from the tragedy unfolding not far from us.'

They went into another short silence, broken only by the squeals and shouting from the children playing around them.

'I'm sorry, what is your name again?' Yvette asked.

'Craig Williams.'

Craig offered his hand and Yvette took it, igniting a feeling of familiarity between them. Then, Craig started to shake a little. He withdrew his hand and closed his eyes, staying like that for a while. Eventually he opened his eyes and smiled. They drifted into a silence, which was finally broken when Craig spoke up.

'I must confess that I have noticed you here before, but I lacked the courage to introduce myself.'

'Oh, I see. Well, there is nothing to be afraid of. I'm a simple girl really.'

They both returned to eating their lunches and drifted into silence. Yvette finished her lunch first and stood up. She was about to take her leave when Craig spoke up.

'May I see you again, Yvette?'

'Well, I …'

'Please. I don't have many friends in Paris and I would like you to become one.'

'Well, like I say, I come here often. If we meet again, I would be pleased to chat.'

Craig smiled and thanked her. Yvette returned his smile and left.

After she had gone, Craig felt foolish. Yvette had offered him so much information about herself, and he had revealed so little of himself. He thought about what she had said, and a wave of sympathy passed over him. He wished there were something he could do for her. *Never mind,* he told himself. He would come to the park at the same time each day until he saw her again.

Yvette too, had noticed Craig in the congregation at church. She was taken by his confidence, which paradoxically seemed to be tempered by a sense of vulnerability. At times he seemed so calm, yet he sometimes also trembled and shook. *Strange*, she had thought. *Why did he do that?* Yvette had wanted to ask him what had happened, but she felt she would be intruding. She began to wonder if getting involved with Craig would only further complicate her life, but something in the young lieutenant's face drew her to him. She had told him she was simple. *Am I really that simple?* Yvette thought. *How would I explain Charles?*

The next day, Craig was at the park again, looking for Yvette. He was not disappointed. She saw him and walked over.

'I see you have returned,' Yvette said, standing confidently in front of him.

Craig stood up, smiled and took her hand.

'Yes, I was hoping to see you again,' he replied, then gestured for her to sit down. They sat for a while smiling at each other.

'There are some things I need to tell you, Craig.'

'Yes, I guess there are a lot of things we need to share.'

Yvette didn't hesitate and pushed on.

'I am married, but my husband has been listed as missing in action for over a year now. I guess he will not be coming back to me.'

There was regret in her voice, tempered with a realism of her situation. She had come to accept the position she was in. She went on to tell Craig of her relationship with Charles. She said that Charles had looked after her well when she was in desperate need of having someone she could rely on. She went on to say that Charles had told her that he intended to separate from his wife and join her in Paris after the war.

She paused here and sighed, then went on. She said that she didn't know what to do, because she felt sorry for Charles' wife, and was not at all sure that she wanted to live with Charles indefinitely. She felt that she owed him for looking after her but was not sure that she wanted to spend the rest of her life with him.

Again, she paused. Perhaps now Craig would not want to be friends with her, but she still felt drawn to him—like there was something there between them. She fell silent, waiting for Craig to say something.

Eventually, Craig turned to face her.

'I would cherish your friendship, Yvette. Even if you

choose to stay with Charles, I would still enjoy seeing you whenever I could. You know, I have been touched by this war as well. My nerves are not what they once were and now I have to control these shakes that I get every now and then.'

'Yes, I noticed that. What causes it?'

'That's a long story, but I have received treatment, and am now doing reasonably well. They only appear now whenever I am anxious or nervous. Once we become better friends, I am confident they will disappear altogether. That said, would you like to go out to dinner with me tonight?'

'Knowing what you do about me, are you sure you want to?' she asked.

'Very much,' Craig replied.

Yvette smiled and gazed into Craig's eyes. She couldn't help but feel drawn to him.

'I would be pleased to go to dinner with you, Craig.'

They arranged a meeting and then sat quietly, each absorbed in their own thoughts.

Yvette wondered what Craig must think of her, but she could not resist the emerging feelings she had for him. Yvette felt relaxed around Craig, which was something she had never felt around Charles.

'I hope we can see a lot more of each other in the coming months,' Craig said.

'I hope for the same thing,' Yvette replied.

'You know this war is coming to an end. The Germans have already made overtures for a peace settlement. People will have to start making arrangements for living in peace.'

Yvette was taken aback.

'How do you know that?' she asked.

'When you work in an embassy, you can learn a lot if you keep your ears and eyes open. Now that the Americans have joined with us, the Germans know that they cannot win this war, and their home front is collapsing.'

'I see. How much longer do you think it will be?'

'A matter of months, if not weeks.'

'Goodness, so quick. It doesn't seem possible after so long.'

Yvette's mind raced to her relationship with Charles. She would have to resolve that soon.

* * *

After her eight-week posting to 3CCS in France, Ann was back at the First Australian Auxiliary Hospital in

London. She had left Joan and taken up residence in a boarding house near the hospital. The boarding house was run by a Mrs Wilson, who provided her with a room and three meals daily. Breakfast was between 6:00 am and 7:00 am, lunch between 12:00 midday and 1:00 pm, and dinner was provided between 6:00 pm and 7:00 pm. All meals were only available between these times, so if Ann missed a meal she had to provide for herself. If anyone wanted a cut lunch to take to work, they had to notify Mrs Wilson during the previous evening. Consequently, Mrs Wilson spent most of her day in the kitchen preparing meals.

Visitors were not allowed in the rooms after dark, so if there were any guests, they had to be entertained in the lounge room. A telephone was located in the lounge room, but unless someone was there to take a call, it remained unanswered. All calls out had to be paid for, so a register was located near the phone and tenants were expected to register their calls and settle their account at the end of each month. Mrs Wilson made it very clear that if the honour system did not work, she would have the phone disconnected.

There were three other boarders at the boarding house, all of whom worked at the hospital. Ann enjoyed her stay at the boarding house because of the cheerful presence of other nurses. They were always accessible and frequently offered to help Ann in any way they could. Ann, of course, reciprocated their help. Mrs Wilson, although a stickler for the rules, was nevertheless a kind-hearted woman. Besides, Ann understood the necessity for rules, having run her own ward for some two years.

On this occasion, Ann returned home early, having been on the midnight-to-dawn shift. She carried Peter's letter with her. It had taken a long time for the letter to reach the hospital and she was eager to read it. She sat down on a chair in her room near the window and opened her letter. After reading it, she smiled to herself. It was such a delight to get letters of appreciation from previous patients, and Peter's letter was punctuated with his thanks to her.

Peter's letter left Ann in a dilemma, however. On the one hand, she had only just separated from Charles and valued the freedom and independence that had given her; while, on the other hand, she liked Peter and knew that a continued correspondence with him could lead to more than just friendship. Nevertheless, she knew that she would have to reply and provide him with a return address. Since it had taken so long for Peter's letter to reach her, she decided to reply immediately.

In her letter, she told Peter that she was happy to have helped him and how delighted she was to learn that he was doing so well. She explained that her reply was delayed because his letter had only just found her. She commented on how glad she was that he had found a posting in Monash's HQ and that he was happy with his work. She went on to say how difficult it was at the CCS, dealing with patients with raw wounds from the front and how it had affected her, but she realised that he had to deal with that as well. Finally, she told Peter about her separation from Charles, and how she was sad at first but was now beginning to enjoy her new-found freedom. She left it at that, not wanting to go into her separation in any detail.

She sealed the envelope and walked to the nearby post office to post it. She enjoyed the walk. The regular steps and fresh air helped settle her mind. She hoped Peter would respond to her letter; after all, she told herself, she was a free woman now, and enjoyed the attention Peter was showing her.

* * *

Craig and Yvette had been seeing each other for two weeks. They had shared many stories and always smiled when they were together. This particular night, Craig sat in a quiet restaurant not far from the Embassy, waiting for Yvette to arrive. He was happy when she finally appeared, and he stood up, holding her chair for her to be seated.

'Thank you for coming tonight,' Craig said.

'We had agreed,' Yvette replied.

'Yes, but I am still happy to see you.'

'I also am happy, Craig.'

They sat down on opposite sides of the table and looked into each other's eyes.

'Have you thought much about what you would do after the war?' Craig asked.

'Not really. That still seems so far away.'

'No, it is coming, I assure you.'

'I see. Well, what do you suggest I do?'

'What skills do you have, Yvette?'

'I have no skills. I married right after school, and I have never even had a job.'

'But you speak English and French.'

'Yes, I suppose that is a skill. I learnt English at school and my English has got better with the war.'

'Do you type?'

'No, I told you, I have no skills.'

'Well, if I paid for you to go to typing school, would you go?'

'Yes, of course. But why do you want me to type?'

'Because the Embassy where I work is always looking for people with typing skills, and your speaking English would be a big factor in getting a job there. Once you can type, I could put in a word for you. I can't guarantee anything mind, but I'm sure they would be interested in you.'

'That's very kind of you. Getting a job would help me so much.'

'Then I will do it. You can start typing school right away. Just find a typing school and let me know how much it costs. I'll also get you an old typewriter from the Embassy so you can practise at home. How may I contact you when I have it?'

Yvette gave Craig her address.

'I'm sorry, I don't have a telephone.'

'That's okay. I'll drop it around as soon as I get it.'

'How long does it take to learn how to type?' Yvette asked.

'That depends on you—how committed you are, but

I'm sure you will learn fast.'

'Why are you doing this for me?' Yvette asked, a puzzled look crossing her face.

'Because I care for you. I am sorry you have had such a bad deal from this war, and I want to help.' Craig smiled, and Yvette returned it with a smile of her own. The meal arrived and they ate while chatting about small things. Craig felt sure that Yvette's self-confidence would grow once she had a job. Maybe then she could make decisions for herself, instead of relying on others to make them for her.

Peter was sitting at his desk compiling his latest report when Major Smith entered the HQ and asked his staff to gather around him.

'Well, gentlemen, I have some great news. The Germans have surrendered and will sign an armistice in November. In fact, the war will end on the eleventh hour of the eleventh day of the eleventh month. We are all hoping that the significance of this day will help put an end to all modern-style warfare, which results in such terrible casualties.'

There was silence all around as the soldiers in the HQ tried to digest what they had just heard. Could it really be true—an end to this terrible war, after such a long time and so many casualties? Could it really be true? Then one soldier started to clap, followed by another then another, until all those present broke out in cheering and applause.

The Major waited for the cheering to die down before he went on.

'We all have to remember that the war will not come to an end until the designated time. Consequently, we must all be vigilant until then. I'm sure the Germans will continue in their belligerent way until the very end, so please be careful, and remind all our soldiers to do the same.'

There was silence again, until this new perspective sunk in—what it meant for them and all those on the front.

How unfortunate it would be for soldiers to become casualties between now and November, Peter thought. No doubt some will continue to prosecute the war until the very end. Therefore, the chief concern for all should be survival, surely.

Peter's mind went immediately to Ann. They had been corresponding now for some weeks and Peter had come to believe that there was something more than just friendship between them. It was clear that Ann valued her independence, but he thought that could be maintained despite a growing affection between them.

What Peter would have to do now was to find some

way to stay in Europe, where he could be near Ann. Since he had been working in Monash's HQ and compiling reports, he had come to believe that he might have a future with his writing. He knew that the Australian Government needed reports from their embassies. Perhaps he could find employment in one of them. He had been thinking about this for some time now and thought he might ask Major Smith for his approval to make an application with them. He decided to raise this possibility with the major while he was present, and after the staff had dispersed and returned to their duties.

'Excuse me, Sir. I would like to speak to you about my future after the war,' Peter said.

'Yes, Peter. How may I help?'

'I would like to stay in Europe after the war and was wondering if I could find employment with one of the Australian Embassies, writing reports for the government.'

'I don't see why not, Peter. After all, you have done such a good job for us. Would you like me to raise this with General Monash?'

'I would be grateful if you could, Sir.'

Major Smith nodded his head and smiled.

'I'll see him and get back to you in the next few days.'

'Thank you, Sir.'

With that said, Major Smith took his leave and Peter went back to his desk to finish his report.

* * *

Yvette had been working at the Australian Embassy as a typist/interpreter (when required) for a couple of weeks, when Charles arrived in Paris on a four-day leave. For some time now, Yvette had been thinking seriously about her relationship with Charles. Now that she was working and earning an income for herself, she began to wonder where she and Charles were heading. How permanent was their relationship, and what did she expect from it? The truth was that she had never expected it to last very long. She always felt that one day Charles would leave her for another woman, just as he had done to his wife; and now that she had an income of her own, she felt liberated enough to raise the issue with Charles.

When she arrived at their apartment, Charles was waiting for her.

He addressed her with thinly-veiled hostility.

'Where have you been?' he asked when she stepped through the door. 'I was surprised that you weren't here when I arrived. It's after five o'clock.'

Yvette didn't like the tone in Charles' voice, so she squared her shoulders, stood erect and narrowed her eyes.

'I've been at work,' she replied.

'I didn't know you had a job. Why do you want to work?'

'I like my job, and it's nice to have money of my own.'

'What do you do anyway?'

'I'm working in the Australian Embassy.'

'Doing what?'

Yvette was annoyed with Charles questioning her. It seemed like an interrogation.

'I type, and sometimes they ask me to interpret for them.'

'The Australians again. My wife works in one of their hospitals, and that changed her. This war has changed so much. It's time for everything to get back to the way it was before.'

'If you are asking me to give up my job, Charles, the answer is no. I have no intention of going back, now that I have something I like.'

Charles seemed surprised that Yvette was so forthright.

'Well ... I ... you could work for me once I get my business started.'

'No, Charles. Like I said, I like my job at the Embassy.'

'I see.' Charles' anger was beginning to show. 'So, you want to be independent. Like my wife.'

'Yes, I suppose I do,' Yvette said defiantly.

'This changes things between us, Yvette. I don't know how independent you want to be, but I would prefer it if you would stay at home and look after things here. For both of us.'

'No, Charles. I don't want that. You are right though—it does change things between us.'

Charles' eyes opened wide and he shook his head. Yvette knew he had not seen this coming. She was angry that he had just assumed she would want the same life he had seen for both of them.

'What changes do you mean?' he said, sitting down on the sofa and crossing his legs.

'I want to get a place of my own.'

'I see. Anything else?'

'I know how good you were to me, Charles,' she said, trying to broach the subject of where their relationship was heading.

'What are you trying to say, Yvette? I thought we had

something special.'

'I know, Charles, I know. But things change.'

'I left my wife for you, you know. You never gave me cause to believe there was anything wrong between us. I thought we would be together for the rest of our lives.'

'Yes, I know. It was like that for me too. But things have changed now.'

'Is there another man? Is that why you want to leave?'

'Yes … no … I mean there is somebody, but we are just friends. I'm sorry, Charles, but I want to move on, and I want to do that by myself. Not with anyone else.'

'I suppose this new man in your life helped you get your job.'

'Yes, he did. But I got the job on my own merit. I did it myself and I want to move on for myself—not for anyone else.'

'I see. Is there anything I can say that would convince you to stay?'

'No, I'm sorry, but I want to be alone for a while.'

Charles' anger snapped. He stood up, reached out and grabbed Yvette by the arm, pulling her towards him.

'You'll never leave me. Do you hear me? You'll never leave me.'

His hold on her tightened. She tried to break free of

his grip, but he held her fast. Then he turned her head with one hand and kissed her hard on the lips. Yvette surrendered to his harsh demand, then broke her lips from his.

'You'll always be mine, Yvette. I'll never let you go. Don't you understand how I feel?'

Yvette finally broke free of Charles' grip and rushed towards the door, but Charles caught her and turned her towards him.

'Where do you think you are going?' he asked between clenched teeth.

'I'm leaving, Charles. Please don't try to stop me. It will only make matters worse for both of us.'

'Do you think I will just let you go? After all I have done for you. Don't you think you owe me more than that?'

Yvette began to feel afraid for her own safety. Charles seemed to be forcing her into a situation from which there was no escape.

'Please, Charles. You are hurting me. I don't want us to part like this. I would like to remember us as being kind to each other. I want the pleasant memories to be the lasting ones.'

'You cheap little slut! You use men to get what you

want, then you drop them. Just like that. I suppose I'm better off without you—now that I know what you're like. Go on then, get out. I don't want to look at you anymore. You disgust me.'

Charles was beginning to calm down. He released Yvette from his grip, and they stood opposite each other.

'Yes, Charles. We would both be better off. We could both make a fresh start.'

Now that Yvette had seen this aggressive side to Charles, she was glad to make a break from him. She realised that they would not have been happy together. One day, she would have challenged his hold on her, and he would have responded with aggression. She had thought that Charles would have been the one to leave her, however, so she was somewhat surprised with the turn of events today. Whatever was to happen now, she was certain of one thing—her relationship with Charles was at an end.

Charles sat back down on the sofa and placed his hands between his knees.

'We're better off without each other and I'm better off finding out what you are really like now, rather than later,' he said.

Yvette nodded her head.

'Yes,' she replied.

'Well, go on then,' Charles said, flinging one arm out, extending it forcefully. 'Get out and don't come back. I don't want anything else to do with you.'

That said, Yvette went into the bedroom and packed her bags. When she returned, she stopped opposite Charles on her way to the front door and looked down at him. She was about to say something in parting, when he turned his face away from her.

'Just go,' he said, shaking his head.

She didn't look back as she left the apartment, and Charles didn't watch her go.

* * *

The last man killed in WWI was George Price, a Canadian soldier serving in 'A' Company, 28th Battalion. He was killed by a German sniper at 10:58 am, on 11 November 1918, just two minutes before the armistice came into effect at 11:00 am. Such was the hostility that still existed in the German ranks.

Now that the war had ended, Peter was compiling his last report, when Major Smith came up to him with good news.

'I spoke to General Monash about your request,

Peter, and he has arranged interviews with *The Age* newspaper as their foreign correspondent, and with the Australian Embassy in London as their liaison officer,' Major Smith said while smiling at Peter. 'A good result I'd say,' he added.

'Yes. Thank you, Sir. Where and when are the interviews to be held?'

'Well, the one for the Embassy is rather urgent, so I have arranged a leave pass for you. You can leave for London as soon as you finish that report you are currently working on. Both interviews will be held at the Australian Embassy in London.'

'They are not wasting any time, Sir.'

'No. Once you are packed, you can take the unit car and driver and have him drop you at the nearest railway station.'

'Thank you, Sir.'

That said, Major Smith left Peter to finish his report.

Four days later, Peter stood inside the Australian Embassy in London, looking down at the receptionist. She gave him directions to the room where the interviews would take place, and not long after that, he was being interviewed for the position at the Embassy.

The interview went well and Peter was told that the position was his, if he wanted it. However, Peter asked if he could wait until the interview with *The Age* was completed before making up his mind. The interviewer said that would be acceptable.

The interview with *The Age* newspaper was not to be held until two days later, so Peter took the opportunity to visit with Ann at the Australian Auxiliary Hospital in Harefield Park. Ann was on a rostered day off, but Peter was given her address by a sister who had known Peter during his time there, and who also knew that Ann would want to see him.

Peter arrived at the boarding house as Ann was taking her lunch, and Mrs Wilson offered to make Peter a sandwich lunch.

'Don't go to any trouble,' Peter said.

'No trouble at all. Nothing is too much trouble for our boys in uniform,' Mrs Wilson replied.

Peter was delighted by Mrs Wilson's response.

After lunch, Peter and Ann took a walk to the nearest park, where they sat beside each other on a park bench.

'It's so good to see you again, Ann. I feel that I know so much about you now from our letters.'

'Yes, I feel the same way, Peter.'

'You know, I might get a job here in London now that the war is over. I'm actually here at the moment having interviews for positions.'

'Oh. Well, that would be good. Are you sure you want to stay in London? What about your family back home?'

'Yes, I will miss them, but I want to be near you. You must know by now that I am sweet on you.'

Ann smiled and turned her gaze on Peter.

'I had guessed that was the case by your letters,' Ann said.

'Yes. And how do you feel about me?'

'The same, Peter. I'm sweet on you too. But I don't want to keep you from your family back home.'

'Don't worry, Ann. That is a decision I have made. Anyway, I intend to travel home now and then.'

'I see.'

They both smiled at each other. Peter took Ann's hands in his own. They sat like that, looking into each other's eyes for some time. Finally, Peter embraced Ann, and kissed her lightly on the cheek.

'I'm happy that you feel the same way about me,' he whispered in her ear.

Two days later, Peter had the interview with the

representative for *The Age* newspaper. After the interview was completed, he went back to the HQ in France. He didn't know how he went in the interview with the newspaper, but both interviews seemed to go well. He had to do some writing for *The Age* interview, about a fictitious story. However, he remembered the old adage about newspaper stories: 'who, what, where, when and why'. The interviewer seemed impressed with his story, but it was difficult to know how he had done.

When Peter was back at HQ, Major Smith came up to him again.

'You are impressive, Peter. You can take your pick of the jobs. You got both of them!'

'That's good news, Sir.'

'Which one do you think you will take?'

'The one with *The Age*, Sir.'

'Good choice. That means you can start writing for them right away. They want a take on how the front is closing down. You are to follow the 9th Battalion into Belgium and report on their activities. You'll need a by-line, and you can submit your reports through the Embassy here in France.'

'Does that mean I'll be leaving HQ immediately?'

'Yes, that's right, Peter. All the best, old man,' Major Smith said, extending his hand towards Peter. They shook hands and exchanged a smile.

'Thank you for everything, Sir. I really enjoyed working for you.'

'A pleasure, Peter, a pleasure.'

A few days later, Peter was attached to the 9th Battalion awaiting movement into Belgium.

* * *

Yvette took her lunch with Craig, as was usual for them, at a café near the Embassy. She was anxious to tell him that she was now living alone.

'Craig, I left Charles,' she said.

'I see. Well, I'm pleased you did.'

'Yes, I'm living near the Embassy. I have a room in a boarding house.'

'That's handy.'

'Yes, I walk to work each morning. You live near the Embassy too, don't you?

'Yes, that's right, and for the same reason you do—so I can walk to work.'

They went silent, concentrating on their ham and cheese croissants coupled with hot coffee. It was a cold

November day, so the coffee warmed their hands and insides.

Eventually, Yvette broke the silence.

'Charles was very upset with me,' she said.

'Did he hit you?'

'No, but he made threats.'

'Is there anything I can do?'

'No, everything is fine,' Yvette lied.

She really wanted to ask Craig if she could move into his apartment, as she was still unsure what Charles was capable of, but she didn't know how Craig would react to such a request, so she said nothing.

They went silent again, each of them absorbed in their own thoughts. Craig placed his hand on the edge of the table, moving it back and forth along the table's edge.

'Now that Charles has gone, would you like to go out with me one night?' he asked.

'I would like that very much, Craig,' Yvette replied.

'Would this Saturday be good for you?'

'Saturday would be fine.'

When Saturday evening came, Craig stood nervously outside the house where Yvette was boarding, waiting for her to appear. When she did, he was struck by her beauty. Her hair had just been washed and it shone in the lamp light; her makeup highlighted her eyes, giving them an exotic quality; and her dress was tight-fitting, with a wrap hanging off her shoulders.

'Wow!' Craig exclaimed. 'You look beautiful, Yvette.'

Yvette smiled. She walked up to Craig and placed her arm in his.

'And you are a handsome man,' she said, smiling up at him. 'Where are you taking me tonight?'

'I thought we could go to a cabaret. Would you like that?'

'That would be fine.'

They walked to the Champs-Élysées, where they hailed a Hansom cab. There were taxicabs they could have taken, but Craig opted for the more romantic Hansom cab. As the horse clip-clopped along the paved street, Craig slipped his arm around Yvette's waist, and she slid over close to his side.

The cabaret they arrived at had a band playing with a young woman singing. Most of the patrons were absorbed in conversation, ignoring the live show. Smoke hung heavy in the closed room and some of the patrons were already beginning to shout and gesticulate, showing the first signs of drunkenness.

Craig turned to Yvette, who wrinkled her nose, so he led the way to a quiet restaurant/bar, with a pianist playing softly in a corner. They found a table near a wall not far from the pianist.

Craig was excited over the prospect of sharing the evening with Yvette and was keen to make a good impression. As the evening progressed, they continued to smile and laugh together. When the meal was coming to a close, Craig leaned in close to Yvette.

'What do you want to do now?' he asked.

'We could stay on here if you like. The music is good and I like the atmosphere.'

'Um … Yvette, I would like to be alone with you …'

Yvette looked into Craig's eyes but said nothing, waiting for him to go on.

'I … er … I … Could we go to a hotel?' Craig blurted it out so suddenly that it surprised even himself.

'Do you think we know each other well enough for that? I want our friendship … is that the right word? Something more than that I think …'

'Relationship?' Craig suggested.

'Yes, relationship … I want our relationship to last. I want to be sure before I commit. Does that make sense to you?'

'Yes, I understand. You want me to respect you and you are worried that I will think less of you if you go with me now.'

'Yes, something like that.'

'Yvette, we have known each other for some time now and I do respect you. You have come so far in the last couple of months. You are more independent now.'

'Yes.'

'Believe me, I want more than just one night with you. I too am looking for something that will last.'

'Well, it is the next step I suppose. I was wondering what would happen when we came to this moment.'

'Yes, and what difference does it make if we make it tonight or in a few months' time?' Craig went silent, waiting for Yvette's reply.

Yvette thought about Craig's words, for what seemed like a long silent moment.

'Yes,' she finally said. 'All right. Do you have a place in mind?'

'No, I thought we could ask the cabbie to take us somewhere.'

'Yes, all right. Shall we go?'

Craig asked for the bill and they left right away.

The hotel was a modest establishment, not a grand one. The receptionist was efficient and apparently non-judgmental. She merely took their money and handed them a key. The room had a double bed with a table and wash basin beside it. There was also a tall jug of water and some soap.

When Yvette had sat in the restaurant with Craig, pondering his proposition, she'd wondered if he was being truthful with her or just wanting to sleep with her. Then, she'd felt ashamed of herself for thinking so badly about Craig. After all, he had been so honest and helpful towards her in the past, so she really had little cause to doubt him. Besides, she wanted a night with him just as much as he wanted one with her. *If we sleep together, it will be easier for me to suggest we live together,* she had reasoned to herself.

Craig and Yvette stood looking at each other. Eventually, Yvette smiled and moved up to Craig, who took her in his arms. He kissed her lightly on the lips and she responded by placing her hand on the back of his head, pulling him closer to her. Their breathing became heavier; then Craig lifted her in his arms and carried her to the bed.

Their lovemaking started out soft and tender, then

built to a hard and fast thrusting. Yvette felt the urgency of her emotions and a sudden rush from deep inside her. It caught her by surprise, but she decided to abandon herself to it and enjoy the luxury of its pleasure. Ultimately, the climax came for both of them. Yvette dug her fingers into Craig's back and he held her tightly in his arms. They stayed in each other's embrace, and Craig whispered into Yvette's ear.

'I love you, Yvette. Thank you for tonight, Darling.'

Later, when they were lying on the bed next to each other, Yvette turned on her side, rested her head on her hand and smiled at Craig, who turned his head and returned her smile.

'I hope you won't think I'm too forward, Craig, but I would like to move into your apartment with you.'

'Gosh, Yvette, I have been wanting to ask you to do just that, but I didn't know how to put it to you. I think that is a splendid idea. Yes, yes, please move in with me.'

They both laughed and hugged each other.

* * *

Peter joined the 9th Battalion at Tincourt, just inside the French border. When the armistice became public knowledge, there was much celebration and honking of automobile horns and blowing of trumpets, but back at the battalion, the soldiers wondered what it would all mean for them. Would they now march unopposed all the way into Germany, or would the war simply end for them at their present location? These were the questions which weighed heavily on the soldiers' minds, and it was this human-interest angle that Peter adopted in his reports back to *The Age* newspaper.

The battalion was twice paraded for the purpose of moving off, and twice their orders were cancelled. Of course, this led to a great deal of uncertainty in the ranks. Eventually, they were provided with motor transport, which carried them into Mazinghien, a village that had been occupied by the Germans, who had removed all stocks of food and clothing prior to their retreat. The village had also been extensively damaged by the war, and consequently, the Allied troops were trying to respond to the local population's needs.

On November 13th, there was a brigade parade, where the soldiers were addressed by General Gordon Bennett, who officially informed them that the war was over and congratulated them on their victory. He also informed them that they would not march into Germany.

The following day, the battalion marched into Bohain, a fairly large town in France, which had not seen much of the destruction of the war. However, the townspeople were practically starving, so the first hot meal that the 9th received was shared equally with the local people. These were the types of stories that Peter wrote about, and there was no shortage of stories for him about the goodwill that existed between the soldiers of the 9th and the local inhabitants.

After several weeks of following the 9th and its activities, Peter was recalled to London, where he was expected to cover the political aspects of the German surrender and the reaction on the home front. Now that he was back in London, he took the opportunity to visit with Ann, and he even wrote a report about the winding down of activities in the First Australian Auxiliary Hospital. In fact, he also reported on how the armies in France were simply melting away as the troops were demobilised and returned to their homes.

'Hello, Ann. It's good to see you,' Peter said, stepping into the boarding house where Ann stayed. Ann was happy to see him, and smiled broadly as she let him in.

'Hello, Peter. It's good to see you too.'

'I must tell you, I've been permanently posted to

London, so we can see a lot more of each other—if you want.'

'Yes, I'd like that.'

'Can we have lunch together today? I'll take you to some place nearby.'

'Oh, I think we can have lunch here, if you like. Then take a walk afterwards.'

'Would that be all right with Mrs Wilson? She has already broken the rules once for me.'

'Oh, don't worry. She likes you.'

They took their lunch in the kitchen and enjoyed the company of a cheerful Mrs Wilson. After lunch, they took a silent walk together where Peter took Ann's hand in his. Ann responded by moving up close to Peter's side, their thighs touching. Then Peter stopped in the same park they had visited before.

'Ann, you do know how much I care for you, don't you?'

'Yes, Peter. And I feel the same about you, but what can we do about it? I have my career and I'm still married to Charles.'

That was the first time that Ann had used Charles' name, and it hit Peter like cold water in the face.

'But you said your marriage was over—that you and

Charles had agreed to live separate lives.'

'All that is true, and I fully intend to live apart from Charles, but I will still be a married woman.'

'Yes, I know that Ann, but do you want to spend the rest of your life without someone special in it?'

'No, I don't. I guess I'm just asking you for some time. I'm not ready just yet to become involved in an intimate affair.'

'I can understand that. Take as much time as you want.'

Peter then gave Ann his address in London and asked her to come visit with him anytime.

The next day, Ann stood in Peter's apartment, looking out on a view of the River Thames.

'This is a very nice place,' Ann said.

'Yes, I like it here, but there is one thing missing—you.'

Ann smiled. She had to admit that she would like to move in to Peter's apartment, but she felt things were moving too fast. Then she remembered that Peter and she had known each other for over a year now, and it was a year where they had learned a great deal about each other, but she wondered how much of her present independence she would have to give up for Peter.

'Would you let me come and go as I please?' Ann asked.

'Well, sure. But I am still talking about an exclusive relationship, Ann.'

'Yes, I would want that too. You exclusive to me as well as me to you.'

'Of course.'

The last of Ann's concerns had been removed. She felt reassured. But still, she fought against making a commitment.

'I must admit that I would like to live here with you, Peter, but in truth I want my career too. I have just now got a job as a sister in a North London general hospital. I want to get a room nearby the hospital, so I can be on call whenever they want me. So, you see, I can't live with you here. All I can offer is moments snatched now and then. Are you sure that will be enough for you?'

'I'll take whatever I can get, Ann. You see, I have fallen in love with you, so there is no one else for me now.'

Peter took Ann in his arms and kissed her on the mouth. She responded by wrapping her arms around him, holding him tightly.

'I have wanted this moment for so long, Ann.'

Craig arrived home late from the Embassy because he'd carried out a late inspection of the Embassy guard. An Australian member of Parliament was to visit the next day, and Craig wanted his guard to be well turned out.

After arriving home, he found Yvette somewhat shaken.

'What seems to be the problem?' Craig asked.

'I think I just saw my husband,' Yvette replied.

'Where?'

'He was standing outside, on the other side of the road, looking at our apartment.'

'Are you sure it was him?'

'I was certain at the time, but now I don't know. He has gone anyway, so it couldn't have been him.'

* * *

In truth, it *was* Yvette's husband. He had been taken prisoner by the Germans and sent to Halle in the southern part of Saxony. When he attempted to escape, he was recaptured and sent to the front, where he joined working gangs for the Germans. His work included digging trenches and constructing dugouts. He was also detailed on burial gangs, where he had to dig mass graves and dump dead bodies into the large pits. He was brutalised by the German soldiers for his efforts—often receiving beatings for the smallest of infractions, like talking or taking too long on a drink break.

Because he was posted to a forward reprisal camp so soon after capture, and because the survival rate for reprisal camp inmates was so low, the German authorities never notified the French Government of his capture.

Life in the reprisal camps was not easy. Although he was an officer, Michel received no special treatment; the fact that he had tried to escape meant that he had to endure what every other POW at these camps had to endure. Life for soldiers sent to reprisal camps was so harsh that many of them died. Those who lived did so on an inadequate diet and long hours of painful work.

Their eyes were hollow, their cheekbones jutting out, and their bodies emaciated. The German soldiers at these camps cared little for the POWs, and often beat them and starved them. Some of the guards drank too much and in their drunkenness often beat the POWs severely.

As a consequence of his diet, Michel had developed digestive problems that would last for the rest of his life. Now that he was back in Paris, he often had bouts of diarrhoea, which left him curled up in pain. The only escape from the pain and his memories of torture was found in alcohol, so he was often drunk and belligerent.

He had learnt from friends that Yvette worked at the Australian Embassy, and had waited for her to finish work, so he could follow her home. He had intended to see her, but something in her demeanour left him standing outside the apartment. He knew she had taken up with an Australian officer from the Embassy, so he decided to wait until they were together, thus enabling him to confront both of them at the same time.

He was angry that Yvette had not waited for him until the end of the war, and his anger towards her increased as he contemplated what the future would hold for them. Would she come back to him, or would she want to stay with this Australian?

He knew he should tell Yvette that he had survived the war, but just walking up to her when she was alone seemed wrong, so he'd left, all the while knowing that he would have to return.

The next day, he again stood outside Yvette's apartment, and again Craig was not with her when she returned. Craig had to attend a party given in honour of an Australian member of Parliament, who had been sent to inspect the Embassy the next day. Yvette started to walk up the stairs of their apartment, then she stopped, turned, and stared at the man on the other side of the street. *Was that my husband?* she wondered. She crossed the road and walked up to him. Michel stood his ground, saying nothing.

'Bonjour, Michel. C'est toi, n'est-ce pas?' she said, furrowing her brow.

Michel stared at Yvette, his face expressionless.

'Yes, it is me, Michel. Your husband.' He replied in French.

'Goodness, Michel. How have you been?'

'Since I found out you have deserted me, how do you think I feel?'

'But I thought you had died a long time ago.'

'No, Yvette. I survived. I was captured by the Germans.'

'I don't know what to say,' she said, a tremor mounting in her voice.

'I want to hold you, Yvette.'

'Yes, of course.'

Yvette moved up to Michel, and he put his arms around her and hugged her for a long time. Yvette felt uncomfortable, like she wanted to escape from his grip. She could smell the alcohol on his breath, and she worried that he might become violent, so she stayed still while he continued to hug her. Eventually, she tried to break free of his grip, but he kept on holding her. He put his hand behind her head and forced it down on his shoulder. Then he took her head in his hands and kissed her roughly on the lips. Yvette took a backward step, breaking away from Michel's grasp.

'I guess you know that things have changed for me. I'm working now and earning a living.'

'Yes, and you're living with someone else.'

'Yes, I needed to survive, Michel, and he has been so helpful.'

Michel went on, ignoring her explanation. 'He is an officer from the Australian Embassy.'

'Yes.'

Yvette didn't know what else to say. She stood still, an awkward silence falling over them. Eventually, Michel spoke up.

'What does that mean for us, Yvette? I still love you. The memory of you was one of the things that kept me alive. Are you going to come back to me?'

Again, Yvette stood silent, not knowing what to say in answer to that question. Finally, she spoke.

'I'm confused, Michel. I've only just now realised that you are alive. I need time to think this out.'

'You should know, Yvette. You should know if you still love me and want to be with me.'

Michel's tone had become aggressive. He was raising his voice and his face became hostile.

'Yes, you are right. I should know.' Yvette tried to be conciliatory, taking some of the heat out of the moment. Then she went on. 'But I still want time, Michel. I need to talk about this with Craig.'

'But you are my wife, Yvette. You should be with me. Your place is with me.'

'I know all that, Michel, but things have changed since we were married. I won't give up my job at the Embassy, and I have to think of Craig too. He has been good to me and I care for him. I owe him that much at least.'

They talked some more. Michel became more and more aggressive, and Yvette tried to calm him. She could not help but feel trapped by Michel, but still she held out. She would decide for herself if she would return to him. She did not want to be bullied into a decision so quickly.

Finally, Yvette took her leave from Michel and hurried inside the apartment to wait for Craig's return. She wondered how best to break this news to Craig and what she would do about her new situation. Should she return to Michel? Then she thought about how much he had changed. Before, he had been so loving, whereas now he was aggressive and hostile. She knew he wanted her back and she worried what he would do if she did not return to him. Craig, on the other hand, was a lot like Michel had been before the war. He was loving and supportive and she liked living with him. They enjoyed each other's company, doing many things together, like preparing meals and cleaning up.

Finally, Craig arrived home. Yvette was waiting for him at the door. She put her arms around him and kissed him tenderly on the mouth. Craig smiled and returned her kiss.

'Wow! What was that for?' he asked.

'You know how much I care for you, Craig. I just wanted to show you that I love you.'

'Umm … what comes now? The bad news?'

'You know that man who I thought was my husband, Michel?'

'Yes, you saw him only yesterday, right?'

'Yes, well he came back today, and I went over to see him. Craig, he *is* my husband. He was captured by the Germans and released after the war. It has taken him this long to find me.'

'I see, and where does that leave us?' Craig asked, a look of concern crossing his face.

'I know, Craig, I know. I'll have to make up my mind who I want to stay with. My heart is with you now Craig, but my mind says I should return to my husband. Oh Craig, he has changed. He is more aggressive and hostile now. I worry what he will do if I do not return to him.'

'If I may say so, Yvette, that is not a good reason for you to return to him. If you do return to him, you need to be sure that you do it for the right reason. Otherwise, you will be unhappy for the rest of your life.'

'Yes, I know that Craig, but it doesn't make the decision any easier for me.'

'No, it doesn't. But you will have to make up your mind sooner or later and it would be better for you to make it sooner rather than later. Whatever you decide, Yvette, I will accept your decision.'

With that said, Yvette moved up to Craig once again and placed her arms around him. Craig responded by holding her close.

'Just hold me, Craig. Hold me tight. I need you now more than ever.'

* * *

Ann was at home when Joan called on her. Ann had just come off a long, tiring shift and was looking forward to an early night, so she was not prepared for a long discussion.

'What can I do for you, Joan?' Ann asked, her tone bordering on annoyance.

'I want you to know that Charles is back from the war, and he is alone. He has left that woman in Paris and is home now.'

'I see. Is there anything else?'

'Don't you see, Ann? You can come back home now and be with Charles. Everything will be like it was before.'

'It won't be the same, Joan, but did Charles say he wanted me back?'

'He misses you terribly and he is sorry for what has transpired between you.'

'Why does he not come and see me himself?'

'He is suffering, Ann. He just sits around in a very black mood—not talking to anyone—just sitting and suffering. He misses you, Ann, and I am afraid of what he might do to himself if you do not come back to him.'

Ann was amazed that Joan could even suggest that she should return to Charles after all that had happened between Charles and herself and amazed at the fact that she should try to make her feel guilty. The thought that Charles might do something terrible to himself left Ann unmoved. After all, Charles did not offer her the same consideration when he left her. In Ann's mind, it was not a matter of forgiveness, it was a matter of her having to give up the new life she had fought so hard to create for herself. The fact that Charles had cheated on her was of secondary consideration now—now it was more a matter of her freedom.

'I don't see how I can return, Joan. You see, I have my career back now, and I am very happy with my new life.'

'But surely, you must still have feelings for Charles and his suffering.'

'I am sorry to hear about that, of course, but I believe he will get over his situation in time, and I am not going to give up my career.'

'Well, you won't have to, Ann. You can still work at the hospital and come home.'

'That won't work. I have to live near the hospital, so I can be on call.'

'Why are you so stubborn, Ann? Don't you love Charles anymore? Your old life is waiting for you. All you have to do is make the move back home. There is so much more in that than caring for sick people in a hospital.'

'I don't see it that way. I get a lot of reward out of caring for the sick and injured. Besides, I have moved on from Charles and my old life. There is someone else in my life now.'

Joan sniffed loudly, sat upright in her chair, and pursed her lips.

'So, you have another man now?'

'Yes, I have. He is understanding about my career, and together we are happy. So, you see, if I was to return to Charles, it would only mean that my new man would be the one to suffer.'

'Well yes, I see that, but you are still married to Charles, and he wants you back. What would we have to do to get you back, Ann?'

'I don't want to come back, Joan. Now that I am an independent woman, I want to remain that way.' There was a finality in Ann's tone that stopped Joan from further pleading Charles' case. She clearly wanted to give vent to her anger towards Ann but stopped herself and took the more diplomatic course.

'I'm sorry to have to tell you this, Ann, but Charles actually wants a divorce. He knows all about Peter and has had a private detective follow the two of you for some time. He has photos of the two of you together and a record of your meetings. He intends to file for a divorce on the grounds of your adultery, and name Peter as your lover.'

Joan stared at Ann, waiting for a response, but Ann simply stared back.

'Oh, Ann,' Joan went on, 'I would still much rather see you and Charles reconcile and get back to the old life that you had before that terrible war started. You know I believe everything you and Charles have been through is a result of the war. Won't you please reconsider?'

Ann was taken by surprise by what Joan had told

her. She placed her elbow on the table separating them, and her hand on her forehead. She thought about all that Joan had said to her. Did Joan really believe all she had said, or was she just anxious about her social standing? Did Charles really want her back, or did he just tell Joan to inform her about his intentions to divorce? Was much of what Joan said just a lie? Was the only truthful thing she said the fact that Charles wanted a divorce?

Ann took her arm from the table, lifted her head, and looked Joan straight in the eye.

'Look, Joan, I'm happy that Charles wants a divorce, and I don't care if he names me as an adulterer, despite the fact that he was the one who cheated on me first. I am happy that I will finally be free of all this and I'm looking forward to being a single woman again, in charge of my own destiny.'

Joan dropped her head and gazed at the table, a long silence resting between them. Finally, she lifted her head and said softly, 'I don't understand young people these days. Women want to work and be independent, not caring about any family responsibility, and men want to divorce themselves from their responsibilities. I read in the paper the other day that the divorce rate has jumped since the war ended. What is happening? Where will it all end?'

Joan went silent, and a sad expression crossed her face. For the first time since she had known her, Ann felt genuine sympathy for Joan. She actually wanted to put her arms around Joan and tell her that everything would be all right, but knew that if she did, Joan would only press her again to return to Charles, and there was no way that was going to happen—not after all this. So, she sat in silence, waiting for Joan to accept her decision.

'Well, keep an open mind, Ann,' she eventually said, 'and if you should want to come back in the future, you know where you can find us. I really would like to see you back home, Ann. A marriage is a sacred thing and you and Charles could make a good couple, as you have done in the past. A love lost can be a love rediscovered.'

* * *

It was a Saturday morning that started out like any other Saturday morning. Craig left for the Embassy early, so he could inspect the changing of the guard. He would be gone for most of the day. Yvette rose late, made herself a coffee, and drank it with a hot croissant. It wasn't long before her mind drifted to the problem that had been plaguing her for the last few days. What was she going to do—return to Michel or stay with Craig?

She had seen Michel twice over the past few days, and each time she saw him he was heavily intoxicated and had become more and more belligerent, insisting that she leave Craig and return to him. He would demand that she return to him, clutching at her arms and putting his face close to hers. He often spoke to her through clenched teeth.

On her part, she had smiled and tried to calm him, telling him that she still needed more time and that she had not yet made up her mind. She knew now that she could not keep this up any longer because Michel was becoming desperate and might do something violent. It was an awful situation for Yvette to be in, but she knew that she had to make an end of it with either Michel or Craig. She was worried about what Michel would do if she told him that she wanted to stay with Craig. Nevertheless, that was the way she was leaning, because she could not see a future for herself with Michel. He had changed so much during the war that she felt she no longer knew him.

She left the apartment around 11:00 am and walked to clear her mind. It was not long before she came to the church where she worshipped on Sundays. She went inside. It was cool and dark, with a statue of Jesus on a cross in front of her. She knew he had suffered so much on her behalf. She knelt at one of the pews and began to pray for guidance. Her mind went to her wedding vows—when she had promised Michel that she would stay with him 'in sickness and in health, for better or for worse'. She knew what the church teachings would tell her to do—she had a duty and a responsibility to Michel.

She paused in her thoughts and looked around. The church now seemed like a solemn place—a cold, unemotional place. She felt she wanted something more cheerful in answer to her sincere inquiry—something she could find hope in. The church had provided her with a solution to her problem, but it was a solution requiring a great deal of sacrifice on her part. Again, she looked at the statue of Christ on the cross. Was this the life she wanted for herself—the life of a martyr?

She left the church and walked to the Eiffel Tower, where she sat in the park. Pigeons came up to her looking for food but she had none to give them, so they soon left her for someone more obliging. The park was a more cheerful setting than the church had been. Here, couples walked hand in hand or arm in arm. They smiled at each other and occasionally kissed. This place was a place of happiness; a place that was bright and full of life, where the sun shone on those below, warming them and cheering them. She began to yearn for such a life; a life full of contentment and goodwill. She believed that such a life could be hers with Craig. She realised that she wanted Craig but that her duty fell with Michel.

She walked back to the apartment, where Michel waited for her on the steps.

'Get your things. You're coming with me,' he said venomously. 'I've had enough of this nonsense. You're making a fool of me, and now you're coming home.'

Yvette was not surprised. She had thought Michel would become violent sooner or later, and now he had come to her after drinking too much, making demands of her, over which she would have no say. If she went with him now, she saw that this pattern would repeat itself.

'I wanted to tell you that I have decided to stay with Craig. I'm sorry, but my future lies with him now.'

'That's where you're wrong,' Michel said, pulling a flick-knife from his pocket and flicking it open. He stepped up close to her and held the knife against her throat. 'Come with me now or die here on the street,' he whispered into her ear.

Yvette was shocked by Michel's sudden action. It had all happened so fast that she had had no time to react. What could she do? She would have to go along with him for now, otherwise she was sure he would make good on his threat.

'Yes, of course, Michel. I'll come with you, but I need to get my things out of the apartment.'

He dropped the knife from her throat and pointed it towards her side.

'All right then. We'll both go.'

Yvette opened the apartment door. Her hand shook as she inserted the key and turned it. They both stepped inside.

'Don't try anything foolish,' Michel said, as he dropped the knife from her side.

They walked up to the bedroom, where Yvette began packing her things into a bag. Then she stopped packing and turned to face Michel. She had decided to confront him. If she went with him now, she would be trapped into a life she did not want.

'I don't want to go with you, Michel. I don't love you anymore. I'm sorry, but that is the way it is. If I go with you now, I'll only run away the first chance I get.'

Michel stepped up to Yvette, pointing the knife at

her abdomen.

'You are coming with me. Now get the rest of your stuff,' he said, pointing the knife towards the bag on the bed, and away from Yvette's abdomen.

Yvette moved quickly and kneed Michel hard in the groin. He dropped the knife, clutching where the blow had struck. Yvette tried to push past him, but he grabbed her by the neck, forcing her to the floor, where he continued to choke her.

Yvette was in a panic. She gasped for air, but Michel only tightened his grip. She tried to push him off, but he was too strong. She turned her head in an attempt to loosen his grip, but he kept choking her.

Then, she saw the knife. It was to her left and within reach. She grabbed it and plunged it into Michel's side. His grip loosened and she stabbed him again in his side. He let go of Yvette's neck, reached around to his side, and sat upright on her stomach. Yvette changed the knife to her right hand and stabbed him in the neck, severing his jugular vein. Blood spurted out in great gushes all over Yvette. Michel reached for his neck to try and stem the bleeding, so Yvette struck again. This time, she struck his chest, puncturing his lungs. She struck over and over again—in his side, in his stomach, in his chest. Eventually, Michel let go and slumped forward onto her. She rolled him off and stood up. There was blood everywhere; all over the floor, and over her clothes. She stood over Michel, knife still in hand, dripping blood. What should she do now, she wondered?

Peter's main focus as foreign correspondent, following the end of WWI, was on political and social issues facing the English people. England had been left with a debt of 130 per cent of its gross domestic product, with America being its main creditor. Lloyd George (England's Prime Minister) had promised to make the Germans pay for England's cost of waging WWI. Working women were forced to surrender their jobs to returning soldiers, and married women were not permitted to work in the government sector. Ambitious reform packages, including public housing and health schemes, were rejected on the grounds of paying down the huge public debt.

There was some progress, however. For example, the Representation of the People Act of June 1918 gave the vote to all men over the age of twenty-one and all women over the age of thirty. Such were the issues that Peter had taken up in his column for the newspaper he wrote for in Australia.

At this precise moment though, he stood alone in his apartment awaiting the arrival of Ann. The two of them had become very close and were now seeing each other on a regular basis. Ann would come to Peter's apartment twice a week, and they would venture out together on Saturday evenings, when Ann's shift work permitted. Peter was lucky with his job at *The Age*, because it provided him with flexible working hours, which meant he could meet with Ann at whatever time her shift work allowed.

There was a knocking on his door, which he recognised as Ann's. She had this rhythmic knock, which was unmistakable. Peter opened the door and immediately embraced Ann, who responded with an embrace of her own.

'So good to see you again,' Peter said.

'Yes,' Ann replied.

Peter closed the door and kissed her. The kiss lingered between them. Then Peter took Ann by the hand and led her to the bedroom.

An hour later, they emerged from the apartment to take dinner at a local restaurant.

'How have you been?' Ann asked, as she glanced through the menu.

'Well. And you?'

'Well. I'm so happy to be here with you,' Ann said, reaching for Peter's hand.

'Ann, we have been doing this for some time now. Do you think we could move in together?'

'We have been through this, Peter. I thought you were happy with our arrangement.'

'I am, I am, Ann. I'm happy, but I want so much to see you more often.'

'And I do too, Darling, but now that my divorce is in its final stage, I'm in no hurry to remarry. I actually cherish my freedom now. Please let me enjoy it for a little longer at least.'

Ann realised that she might have hurt Peter's feelings with her forthrightness, so she tried to console him.

'I do love you, Peter, and I want so much more for us, but for now, I don't want to get married. I'm sorry, Peter, but this is the best I can offer you. I hope you understand because I do not want to lose you.'

'Wait a minute, Ann. Who said anything about losing

each other? Of course I want to stay with you. I love you, Ann, and nothing will ever change that. I just thought we could try to find a way of seeing each other more often.'

A silence arose between them.

'I could come to you three times a week instead of two.' Ann suggested. 'Would that make a difference for you?'

'That would be great,' Peter responded, eagerly embracing Ann's attempt at compromise.

They had to leave that hanging between them, as the waiter arrived and took their order. After he had gone, Peter turned to Ann.

'I don't want to lose you, Ann. Please don't think I'm pressuring you. I understand your position, and I respect it.' Peter smiled, then went on. 'You don't begrudge me for trying to see more of you, do you?'

'No, but like I said, I want to remain single for a while longer. You know that the politicians insist that married women can't work for the government. So, if I get married, I'd have to give up my career at the hospital, and that would be a big sacrifice on my part, as I enjoy my work so much.'

She paused for a moment, her mind racing for a solution that didn't come.

'Oh, Darling,' she eventually said. 'We are in something of a pickle, aren't we?'

Peter nodded his head in agreement.

'Yes. Yes, we are,' he said.

* * *

Yvette returned from the Embassy and went straight for a drink. She poured herself a shot of whiskey, knocked it back, and then poured herself another, before sitting on the lounge sofa. She stretched out her legs and leaned well back, making her body as stiff as a board. Then she relaxed and took a sip of the whiskey.

She had endured a bad day at work. The newspapers were full of the fact that she had killed her husband, and they had even published a photo of her. Her co-workers had been watching her all day. They never said anything to her—never asked how she was. They just stared at her, and this had unnerved her. *Why won't they speak to me?* she asked herself. *Do they think I'm a killer and not worth speaking to?* She also wondered what they said to each other about her when she was not present.

It had all been so terrible. These last few weeks, the papers had covered Michel's death from his point of view. They had pointed out that he had served his country and had endured two years of German captivity, only to return home and be killed by his wife, who was living with another man. They also made reference to the fact that she had stabbed Michel eight times, thereby making sure that she had killed him! The papers questioned whether this was necessary.

They also interviewed a neighbour who lived next door to her when she had been living with Charles. They painted her as a scarlet woman, who had done something disgraceful, thus scandalising her whole life.

All in all, Yvette didn't know what to do next. When she went out with Craig, she would sometimes be stared at, and on one occasion, when she took her lunch alone at the Eiffel Tower, a man had accosted her and shouted abuse at her. She had become so frightened that her hands trembled. So now she only went outdoors with Craig, and even then she worried that he would get into a fight with someone over her, which was something she did not wish to see happen.

Craig came home and sat next to her on the sofa.

'How was your day?' he asked.

'Pretty much as expected. Nobody wants to talk with me, and everyone stares at me. I wish I could get away from it all, but I'll have to stay for the coroner's report.

I might be charged with murder and have to defend myself in court.'

'Well let's hope it doesn't come to that. You still have so much on your side.'

'Yes, but the newspapers don't see any of that. They have already judged me guilty.'

'I know it's hard, but try not to take any notice of that. I'm sure the coroner won't.'

'Well, I hope not, otherwise I'm cooked.'

Craig laughed and took Yvette into his arms and embraced her warmly.

'When all this is over, we can go to Australia, if you like. No one there will know anything about you, and we can start afresh.'

'That would be nice, but I don't want to lose my job here at the Embassy, and if we marry, I won't be able to work anymore.'

The time Yvette had spent with Charles and Craig had improved her English markedly. She had also enrolled in English classes conducted by the Australian Embassy, where she had progressed to the highly competent level with outstanding results. Consequently, she had been transferred out of the typing pool and into the interpreter's section, where she spent most of her time translating documents. She had fought so hard to get ahead in her job and took pride in her achievement.

If she were to go to Australia, there was not much chance of her getting a position interpreting French documents. She also had her eye on the top job in her section here at the Embassy. The current senior interpreter had mentioned that he would like to return to Australia, thus opening up a potential chance for Yvette. So, she did not want to go to Australia, and she did not want to marry Craig, if it meant giving up everything she had worked so hard for.

Craig and Yvette had had this conversation several times, and each time Yvette had told Craig that she did not want to go to Australia, and she did not want to marry him. She preferred to leave things as they were. Craig, on the other hand, had continued to hope that Yvette would change her mind.

They left the conservation hanging between them, as was the usual response when this topic was raised, with Craig wanting them to go to Australia, and Yvette wanting to stay in Paris.

Two months later, the coroner handed down his report. He did not recommend charging Yvette with murder and declared the incident as one of self-defence. He did, however, make one concession on Michel's behalf. He noted that, had Michel succeeded in killing Yvette, he would have been able to defend himself on the grounds of 'crime of passion'.

The police had been busy collecting evidence, and they had discovered facts helpful to Yvette's case.

First, they had questioned those from Michel's neighbourhood who knew him. The police discovered that Michel was almost always drunk and aggressive. He was generally abusive and got into violent fights. The police also discovered that Michel had spoken about killing Yvette, because she had refused to return to him.

Second, the police had traced the flick-knife used in the killing to a local pawnbroker and discovered that Michel had purchased it on the morning of the killing. He had also told the pawnbroker that he intended to force Yvette to come back to him, or he would kill her for treating him so badly. He had said this after the flick-knife was in his possession, otherwise, the pawnbroker said, he would not have sold it to him. But it was too late, and Michel had made a quick departure from his shop.

Third, were the bruises around Yvette's neck, which clearly showed that Michel had tried to strangle her.

The eight stabbings that Yvette had made on Michel could be explained as panic on Yvette's part. After all, Michel was much bigger and stronger than she was.

Yvette took the news with a huge sigh of relief. She would not have to go to court. All this would blow over in a few months, she believed, and return to what it had been like before this terrible incident. She was now hopeful for a bright future in Paris with Craig.

Peter attended the signing of the peace treaty at Versailles, a small village on the outskirts of Paris where King Louis XIV had built his palace. The meeting was held in the Hall of Mirrors and reflected the mood of all those who were meeting on behalf of their countries. Lloyd George, the British PM, set the tone for the Allies with his parting words to the British people: 'I will squeeze the German lemon until the pips squeak.' With such an attitude going into its drafting, the Treaty of Versailles declared that Germany was responsible for starting WWI and therefore responsible for paying all the costs associated with it.

The end result of all this was that Germany would pay reparations to Britain and France, who in turn would pay America for the war debts they had run up, and America, in its turn, would give Germany loans so their economy would not collapse. In this way Britain and France transferred their war debt to Germany.

Billy Hughes, the Australian PM, led a delegation to the treaty, and Craig accompanied that delegation along with several other members of the Australian Embassy in Paris.

It was during one of the breaks in the meeting that Craig ran into Peter, while they were both walking in the immaculate gardens and among the water features of the palace grounds. They recognised each other instantly. Peter opened the conversation.

'Good to see you again, Craig,'

'Yes, what brings you here?'

'I'm covering the peace treaty for my paper back home. I'm a foreign correspondent now. How about you?'

'I'm here with the Embassy staff.'

'I notice you're still in uniform, and an officer to boot.'

'Yes, I'm part of the Embassy guard.'

'I see.'

They went silent after that, both seeming to search their respective memories for something more to say.

'Do you still think of the war?' Craig finally asked.

'I try not to, but you know, it always seems to find a way into my thoughts.'

'Yes,' Craig agreed, his left hand beginning to shake. 'I've had a pretty bad time of it, trying to control my nerves,' he went on. 'Do you ever wonder why we were spared when so many others were not?' A look of genuine concern crossed his face.

'Yes, I guess we all think about that. Were we just lucky not to be standing in the wrong place at the wrong time, or was it something more meaningful? I can't answer that one. I know a lot of good men who died during the war, so it wasn't a case of only those who deserved to die, and it wasn't a case of 'only the good die young', because what would that make of those of us who survived? Were we all the bad ones? I don't think that either. Were we spared for something that we must do now? I don't know about that either, because a lot of us are living ordinary lives—lives that any one of the dead could have led.'

'Yes, it is very puzzling. I can see you have thought a lot about it.'

'Haven't we all?'

'I guess you're right.' Craig paused for a brief moment, then went on. 'I have trouble coming to terms with the fact that I led a lot of young men to their deaths. Do you have trouble with that too?'

'I try not to think about that. It only leads me into depression. Playing the guilt game is not healthy, Craig. You need to get past that, if it is still bothering you.'

'Yes, yes, of course. But how do you get past it?'

'Just let it go, mate. You had a job to do, and you did it to the best of your ability. I know you well enough from when you were my sergeant to know that you were a good leader. The men respected you and looked up to you for guidance. Without you, a lot more would have died. You did a good job, Craig. Don't let it trouble you anymore, mate.'

'Yes, yes, like you say, the men did look to me for leadership. I haven't thought of it like that before. Maybe that can help me get past the guilt.'

With that said, both men slipped into a silence, casting their minds back to a time when they were in the trenches together, wondering if they would make it through the nightmare that was WWI.

www.ingramcontent.com/pod-product-compliance
Lightning Source LLC
Chambersburg PA
CBHW030759190726
48285CB00003B/936